BRACEBRIDGE HALL

BY

WASHINGTON IRVING

WITH ILLUSTRATIONS
BY
Randolph Caldecott

A Facsimile of the First Edition
originally published in 1876
by Macmillan & Company of London

WITH A NEW INTRODUCTION
BY
Andrew B. Myers

SLEEPY HOLLOW RESTORATIONS
Tarrytown, New York

Library of Congress Cataloging in Publication Data
Irving, Washington, 1783-1859.
Bracebridge Hall.

I. Title
PS2057.A1   1978   818'.2'07   78-16387
ISBN 0-912882-35-2

For information, address the publisher:
Sleepy Hollow Restorations
Tarrytown, New York 10591

ISBN 0-912882-35-2
Library of Congress Catalog Card Number: 78-16387

First Printing of The Facsimile Edition, 1978

Manufactured in the United States of America

INTRODUCTION

"Geoffrey Crayon's" second gathering of sketches and tales, *Bracebridge Hall*, came before its transatlantic audience in 1822. Two years before, he had won acclaim with the *Sketch Book*, its medley of English and American materials proving the greatest single triumph for Washington Irving (1783-1859). *Bracebridge*, for all its own lightness and grace, has always stood a little in the shadow of that first lively collection. How could it be otherwise? It had a New Amsterdam "Dolph Heyliger" but he was no Rip Van Winkle, and an Iberian "Student Of Salamanca" but he was no Ichabod Crane. Such literary lightning seldom strikes twice in the same career.

However the new book, subtitled "The Humourists,"* did in full measure display a rich tapestry, woven

* A Paris edition of 1826 reversed the order with, *Les Humoristes, ou Le Chateau De Bracebridge*, by—"Washington Irwing."

in Crayon's inimitable style, of English rural life, and half a century later Macmillan of London chose from the original fifty-odd parts a selection of nearly thirty, to offer a mid-Victorian audience another look at a cherished but gradually vanishing past. To match Irving's familiar word pictures the enterprising publisher chose young Randolph Caldecott (1846-1886) to illustrate this volume, banking on the success of this same pairing, the year before, with *Old Christmas*, five Bracebridge Hall stories taken from the *Sketch Book*. Again the combination worked. This concentrated *Bracebridge Hall*, a return in sequel to other fortunes of the fictitious family and friends, brought together a symbolic John Bull and Brother Jonathan, in one more successful mutual lend-lease of artistic talents.

The Manhattan-born writer, now verily cosmopolitan, described himself in an early chapter here as "a little of a philosopher and a bachelor to boot." This musing spectator's pose was borrowed from established British literary traditions. At the same time, in a preface, not reprinted by Macmillan, Irving spoke jocularly of struggles beforehand to make a favorable impression in London, the literary capital of the English-speaking world. "I was looked upon as something new and strange in literature; a kind of demi-savage, with a feather in his hand instead of on his head, and there was a curiosity to hear what such a being had to say about civilized society."

Part of that society was the "Town" and environs,

and the observant and chatty Crayon wandered much of it in the *Sketch Book*. In *Bracebridge Hall* he was more interested in the "Country," and his long and frequently sentimental look at it is before you, focused on the merry microcosm he dubbed "Bracebridge Hall." Merry, in particular, for though the local first family has both joys and sorrows, this volume ends with wedding bells for the fair Julia and the Squire's son. The neighboring yeomanry, led by robust Ready-Money Jack, are by and large a sturdy lot, though several village eccentrics are appealing exceptions to this rule. Gipsies add an exotic touch, and a tale of thievery.

Where then was, or is, the "real" Bracebridge Hall? Nowhere tangible alas; it never existed in fact. Irving created it in the Made-in-U.S.A. alembic of his imagination, though not without genuine Old World experience to guide him. An indefatigable traveller always, his journeys in England, Scotland, and Wales, amply supplied basic materials to use, now, as literary architect, landscaper, and *pater familias* of the imaginary Bracebridge clan, and its loyal dependents. Nevertheless, even today "originals" are pointed to: for one, the similarly named Barlborough Hall in Cheshire. A bit better claimant seems Aston Hall in Birmingham, preserved now, in close urban surroundings, as a "Country House Museum." In the second floor "Victorian Bedroom" on a night table is, appropriately enough, a copy of *Bracebridge Hall*. Indeed Caldecott, himself thoroughly familiar with the Midlands, thought enough of the pos-

sible connection to use the Jacobean characteristics of
Aston as the model for his Hall, especially in the frontispiece to *Old Christmas*, and that in the present volume,
too.

It seems equally certain there were no complete
originals for the writer's colorful Upstairs-Downstairs
cast of characters. Instead, Irving's searching imagination picked and chose among real people, some known
and some only seen in passing, added a poetic touch or
three, and produced as much clear fiction as fact. We
can be sure, though, on the author's own testimony, that
his memorable visit in 1817 to Walter Scott's baronial
Abbotsford stayed long in mind, and played its part in
creating the senior Bracebridge, and his odd satellite
Master Simon. In 1849, in his Author's Revised Edition
of *Bracebridge*, in a footnote to "English Country Gentlemen," another section not included by Macmillan, Irving
broke silence on the subject:

> The reader who has perused a little work published by the
> author several years subsequently to Bracebridge Hall,*
> narrating a visit to Abbotsford, will detect the origin of
> the above anecdote in the conferences between Sir Walter
> Scott, and his right-hand man, Tommy Purdie. Indeed, the
> author is indebted for several of his traits of the Squire
> to observations made on Sir Walter Scott during that
> visit; though he had to be cautious and sparing in drawing
> from that source.

* *Abbotsford and Newstead Abbey*, the second of three parts in the
Crayon Miscellany (1835).

In this 1877 *Bracebridge Hall*, pristine green cloth and gold-tooled, die-stamped binding, outside, and inside a portfolio of crisp and poignant word sketches, teamed with impressionistic illustrations as often jolly as wistful, the reader at home or abroad got two, so to speak, for the price of one. Such eye-catching book illustration was one of the nineteenth century glories of the burgeoning British publishing industry. This was especially true in the realm of stories for the young, in years or in heart. Randolph J. Caldecott had a hugely successful career as an illustrator of children's books. A contemporary of artists like the formidable Walter Crane and the unique Kate Greenaway, he came to more than hold his own against such competition.

To begin with, however, across the year 1870, he had perforce a kind of apprenticeship to serve, as a contributor of drawings, now to a fashionable periodical like *London Society* and again to the popular press as in the *Graphic*. A natural draftsman, possessed of a clear eye and a sure hand, especially for line, he could add, whether drawing animals or men, a mastery of anatomical detail. And from the start it was obvious Caldecott had a promising vein of humor, a spontaneous sense of the comic which could contribute to telling characterization. Within a decade, indeed immediately after calling much attention to himself by the best-selling duo of *Old Christmas* and *Bracebridge Hall*, he turned to that magical series of books, for moppets on both sides of the Atlantic, which began in 1878 with *John Gilpin's Ride* and *The*

House That Jack Built, and continued steadily until his early demise.

Fair tribute must be paid to Caldecott's own collaborator, in both Irving projects, the masterful engraver James Davis Cooper (1823-1904). Good friends, they matched well each other's spirits and skills, creating thereby new standards. It is reported, "The originals were drawn about one third larger, in pen and ink, photographed on wood, and engraved in facsimile." This method produced a delicate black line texture, as different from the late eighteenth century white line effect with which the remarkable Thomas Bewick triumphed. Today's viewer, the beneficiary of printing techniques undreamed of by Cooper-Caldecott, can still admire their combined artistry in, for example, the *Bracebridge* frontispiece and favorite full illustrations like "The Lovers" (f.p. 43) or contrasting "May-Day Melée" (f.p. 237).

In sum, here in high-stepping tandem are the picturesque anecdotes and sketches of an internationally appreciated storyteller (albeit an American and of an earlier generation) and the legerdemain of an equally gifted young Briton, able to draw with flair and wit. Of the entertaining results one overseas commentator remarked in the 1880s, "for once at least, artist and author were in full accord. These drawings breathe the very spirit of the original and lend a charm even to Washington Irving's delicate humour and sweet and tender fancy."

By these years Irving's name had long since gone before him, as a pioneering professonal of letters in his own land, and an ambassador of goodwill abroad for our young country and culture. This *Bracebridge Hall* of 1877 reached an America where echoes still rang of the republic's Centennial celebrations just the twelvemonth before. One might expect therefore the markedly Anglo-Saxon elements in Irving's volume would have found it hard going over here. It proved not so. Things quite English still had a hold on many native hearts. And Geoffrey Crayon was not writing about the United Kingdom under Queen and Empress, but about once-upon-a-time aspects of an anciently self-sustaining agricultural society, subsequently endangered by the mixed blessings of the Industrial Revolution. Americans could see their own parallels already, and were pleased many of them to lose themselves, for an hour or two, in this almost escapist tour of "long ago and far away." Moreover, note that Irving's mind was not always only on romantic evocations; his humor often had a serious vein in it. Implicit in *Bracebridge Hall* from the beginning was reflection on progress, so-called, as both profit and loss.

In any event, editions of this version multiplied, homegrown and foreign. Inevitably the idea came of combining *Bracebridge Hall* with *Old Christmas* as a gift-book endeavor. In 1886 Macmillan put out, in both London and New York, an *édition de luxe*, with both units in one cover, each exactly reprinted, including the original decorative title pages. The binding was especially handsome, a rich blue, with elaborate gold-tooling, and both Irving's and Caldecott's name on front cover and spine. This royal quarto editon had a page size allowing generous margins, providing comfortable framing for the scores of fascinating pictures. The solemn *Times* of London called the results "cheery almost beyond conception."

The same applies to the present separate edition. For in its turn Sleepy Hollow Restorations has striven to do Space Age justice, in a careful facsimile edition, to the celebrated handiwork of both artists, the writer and the illustrator, all, as you might expect from an institution dedicated to keeping the past as intelligently alive as possible, as a conscious salute to, as Irving's almost last words have it, "good old times." Like quixotic Simon Bracebridge on that closing page (an intriguing character who had a bit of both creators in him) the modern publisher, and your editor, leave you with a wink and a wave. *Bracebridge Hall* is now yours to ramble through. Enjoy!

ANDREW B. MYERS

Fordham University

BRACEBRIDGE HALL

"The chivalry of the Hall prepared to take the field."—*Frontispiece.*

BRACEBRIDGE HALL.

BY WASHINGTON IRVING.

ILLUSTRATED BY R. CALDECOTT.

LONDON.
MACMILLAN & Co.
1877.

Printed by R. & R. CLARK, *Edinburgh*.

THE success of "OLD CHRISTMAS" has suggested the re-publication of its sequel "BRACEBRIDGE HALL," illustrated by the same able pencil, but condensed so as to bring it within reasonable size and price.

DESIGNED BY RANDOLPH CALDECOTT,

AND

ARRANGED AND ENGRAVED BY J. D. COOPER.

———•♦•———

THE HALL.

THE reader, if he has perused the volumes of the
Sketch Book, will probably recollect something of
the Bracebridge family, with which I once passed
a Christmas. I am now on another visit at the
Hall, having been invited to a wedding which is
shortly to take place. The squire's second son,
Guy, a fine, spirited young captain in the army, is
about to be married to his father's ward, the fair
Julia Templeton. A gathering of relations and

friends has already commenced, to celebrate the joyful occasion ; for the old gentleman is an enemy to quiet, private weddings. " There is nothing," he says, " like launching a young couple gaily, and cheering them from the shore ; a good outset is half the voyage."

Before proceeding any farther, I would beg that the squire might not be confounded with that class of hard-riding, fox-hunting gentlemen so often described, and, in fact, so nearly extinct in England. I use this rural title, partly because it is his universal appellation throughout the neighbourhood, and partly because it saves me the frequent repetition of his name, which is one of those rough old English names at which Frenchmen exclaim in despair.

The squire is, in fact, a lingering specimen of the old English country gentleman ; rusticated a little by living almost entirely on his estate, and something of a humourist, as Englishmen are apt to become when they have an opportunity of living in their own way. I like his hobby passing well, however, which is, a bigoted devotion to old English manners and customs ; it jumps a little with my own humour, having as yet a lively and unsated curiosity about the ancient and genuine characteristics of my "fatherland."

There are some traits about the squire's family also, which appear to me to be national. It is one of those old aristocratical families, which, I believe, are peculiar to England, and scarcely understood in other countries; that is to say, families of the ancient gentry, who, though destitute of titled rank, maintain a high ancestral pride; who look down upon all nobility of recent creation, and would consider it a sacrifice of dignity to merge the venerable name of their house in a modern title.

This feeling is very much fostered by the importance which they enjoy on their hereditary domains. The family mansion is an old manor-house, standing in a retired and beautiful part of Yorkshire. Its inhabitants have been always regarded through the surrounding country, as "the great ones of the earth;" and the little village near the hall looks up to the squire with almost feudal homage. An old manor-house, and an old family of this kind, are rarely to be met with at the present day; and it is probably the peculiar humour of the squire that has retained this secluded specimen of English housekeeping in something like the genuine old style.

I am again quartered in the panelled chamber, in the antique wing of the house. The prospect from my window, however, has quite a different aspect from that which it wore on my winter visit. Though early in the month of April, yet a few warm, sunshiny days have drawn forth the beauties of the spring, which, I think, are always most captivating on their first opening. The parterres of the old-fashioned garden are gay

with flowers; and the gardener has brought out his exotics, and placed them along the stone balustrades. The trees are clothed with green buds and tender leaves; when I throw open my jingling casement I smell the odour of mignonette, and hear the hum of the bees from the flowers against the sunny wall, with the varied song of the throstle, and the cheerful notes of the tuneful little wren.

While sojourning in this stronghold of old fashions, it is my intention to make occasional sketches of the scenes and characters before me. I would have it understood, however, that I am not writing a novel, and have nothing of intricate plot, or marvellous adventure, to promise the reader. The Hall of which I treat has, for aught I know, neither trap-door, nor sliding-panel, nor donjon-keep: and indeed appears to have no mystery about it. The family is a worthy, well-meaning family, that, in all probability, will eat and drink, and go to bed, and get up regularly, from one end of my work to the other; and the squire is so kind-hearted an old gentleman, that I see no likelihood of his throwing any kind of distress in the way of the approaching nuptials.

In a word, I cannot foresee a single extraordinary event that is likely to occur in the whole term of my sojourn at the Hall.

I tell this honestly to the reader, lest when he find me dallying along, through every-day English scenes, he may hurry ahead, in hopes of meeting with some marvellous adventure farther on. I

invite him, on the contrary, to ramble gently on with me, as he would saunter out into the fields, stopping occasionally to gather a flower, or listen to a bird, or admire a prospect, without any anxiety to arrive at the end of his career. Should I, however, in the course of my loiterings about this old mansion, see or hear anything curious, that might serve to vary the monotony of this every-day life, I shall not fail to report it for the reader's entertainment.

> For freshest wits I know will soon be wearie
> Of any book, how grave so e'er it be,
> Except it have odd matter, strange and merrie,
> Well sauc'd with lies and glared all with glee.*

* Mirror for Magistrates.

THE BUSY MAN.

A decayed gentleman, who lives most upon his own mirth and my master's
means, and much good do him with it. He does hold my master up
with his stories, and songs, and catches, and such tricks, and jigs you
would admire——he is with him now. JOVIAL CREW.

By no one has my return to the Hall been
more heartily greeted than by Mr. Simon Bracebridge, or Master Simon, as the squire most
commonly calls him. I encountered him just as
I entered the park, where he was breaking a
pointer, and he received me with all the hospitable
cordiality with which a man welcomes a friend to

another one's house. I have already introduced
him to the reader as a brisk old bachelor-looking
little man; the wit and superannuated beau of a
large family connection, and the squire's factotum.
I found him, as usual, full of bustle; with a
thousand petty things to do, and persons to attend
to, and in chirping good-humour; for there are
few happier beings than a busy idler; that is to
say, a man who is eternally busy about nothing.

I visited him, the morning after my arrival, in
his chamber, which is in a remote corner of the
mansion, as he says he likes to be to himself, and
out of the way. He has fitted it up in his own
taste, so that it is a perfect epitome of an old
bachelor's notions of convenience and arrange-
ment. The furniture is made up of odd pieces
from all parts of the house, chosen on account of
their suiting his notions, or fitting some corner of
his apartment; and he is very eloquent in praise
of an ancient elbow-chair, from which he takes
occasion to digress into a censure on modern
chairs, as having degenerated from the dignity
and comfort of high-backed antiquity.

Adjoining to his room is a small cabinet,
which he calls his study. Here are some hanging

shelves, of his own construction, on which are several old works on hawking, hunting, and farriery, and a collection or two of poems and songs of the reign of Elizabeth, which he studies out of compliment to the squire ; together with the Novelists' Magazine, the Sporting Magazine, the Racing Calendar, a volume or two of the Newgate Calendar, a book of peerage, and another of heraldry.

His sporting dresses hang on pegs in a small closet ; and about the walls of his apartment are hooks to hold his fishing-tackle, whips, spurs, and a favourite fowling-piece, curiously wrought and inlaid, which he inherits from his grandfather. He has also a couple of old single-keyed flutes, and a fiddle, which he has repeatedly patched and mended himself, affirming it to be a veritable Cremona : though I have never heard him extract a single note from it that was not enough to make one's blood run cold.

From this little nest his fiddle will often be heard, in the stillness of mid-day, drowsily sawing some long-forgotten tune ; for he prides himself on having a choice collection of good old English music, and will scarcely have anything to do with

modern composers. The time, however, at which
his musical powers are of most use, is now and
then of an evening, when he plays for the children
to dance in the hall, and he passes among them
and the servants for a perfect Orpheus.

His chamber also bears evidence of his various
avocations; there are half copied sheets of music;
designs for needlework; sketches of landscapes,
very indifferently executed; a camera lucida; a
magic lantern, for which he is endeavouring to
paint glasses; in a word, it is the cabinet of a man
of many accomplishments, who knows a little of
everything, and does nothing well.

After I had spent some time in his apartment,
admiring the ingenuity of his small inventions, he

took me about the establishment, to visit the stables, dog-kennel, and other dependencies, in which he appeared like a general visiting the different quarters of his camp; as the squire leaves the control of all these matters to him, when he is at the Hall. He inquired into the state of the horses; examined their feet; prescribed a drench for one, and bleeding for another; and then took me to look at his own horse, on the merits of which he dwelt with great prolixity, and which, I noticed, had the best stall in the stable.

After this I was taken to a new toy of his and the squire's, which he termed the falconry, where

there were several unhappy birds in durance, completing their education. Among the number was a fine falcon, which Master Simon had in especial training, and he told me that he would show me, in a few days, some rare sport of the good old-fashioned kind. In the course of our round, I noticed that the grooms, gamekeeper, whippers-in, and other retainers, seemed all to be on somewhat of a familiar footing with Master Simon, and fond of having a joke with him, though it was evident they had great deference for his opinion in matters relating to their functions.

There was one exception, however, in a testy old huntsman, as hot as a pepper-corn; a meagre, wiry old fellow, in a threadbare velvet jockey-cap, and a pair of leather breeches, that, from much wear, shone as though they had been japanned. He was very contradictory and prag-matical, and apt, as I thought, to differ from Master Simon now and then, out of mere captiousness. This was particularly the case with respect to the treatment of the hawk, which the old man seemed to have under his peculiar care, and, according to Master Simon,

was in a fair way to ruin ; the latter had a vast deal to say about *casting*, and *imping*, and *gleaming*, and *enseaming*, and giving the hawk the *rangle*, which I saw was all heathen Greek to old Christy ; but he maintained his point notwithstanding, and seemed to hold all his technical lore in utter disrespect.

I was surprised at the good humour with

which Master Simon bore his contradictions, till
he explained the matter to me afterwards. Old
Christy is the most ancient servant in the place,
having lived among dogs and horses the greater
part of a century, and been in the service of Mr.
Bracebridge's father. He knows the pedigree of
every horse on the place, and has bestrid the
great-great-grandsires of most of them. He
can give a circumstantial detail of every fox-
hunt for the last sixty or seventy years, and has
a history of every stag's head about the house,
and every hunting trophy nailed to the door of
the dog-kennel.

All the present race have grown up under his
eye, and humour him in his old age. He once
attended the squire to Oxford when he was a
student there, and enlightened the whole university with his hunting lore. All this is enough to
make the old man opinionated, since he finds, on
all these matters of first rate importance, he
knows more than the rest of the world. Indeed, Master Simon had been his pupil, and
acknowledges that he derived his first knowledge in hunting from the instructions of
Christy; and I much question whether the old

man does not still look upon him as rather a greenhorn.

On our return homewards, as we were crossing the lawn in front of the house, we heard the porter's bell ring at the lodge, and shortly afterwards, a kind of cavalcade advanced slowly up the avenue. At sight of it my companion paused, considered for a moment, and then, making a sudden exclamation, hurried away to meet it. As it approached I discovered a fair, fresh-looking elderly lady, dressed in an old-fashioned riding-habit, with a broad-brimmed white beaver hat, such as may be seen in Sir Joshua Reynolds' paintings. She rode a sleek white pony, and was followed by a footman in rich livery, mounted on an over-fed hunter. At a little distance in the rear came an ancient cumbrous chariot, drawn by two very corpulent horses, driven by as corpulent a coachman, beside whom sat a page dressed in a fanciful green livery. Inside of the chariot was a starched prim personage, with a look somewhat between a lady's companion and a lady's maid, and two pampered curs that showed their ugly faces and barked out of each window.

There was a general turning out of the garrison to receive this new comer. The squire assisted her to alight, and saluted her affectionately; the fair Julia flew into her arms, and they embraced with the romantic fervour of boarding-school friends. She was escorted into the house by Julia's lover, towards whom she showed distinguished favour; and a line of the old servants, who had collected in the hall, bowed most profoundly as she passed.

I observed that Master Simon was most

assiduous and devout in his attentions upon this
old lady.   He walked by the side of her pony up

the avenue ; and while she was receiving the
salutations of the rest of the family, he took occasion to notice the fat coachman, to pat the sleek
carriage-horses, and, above all, to say a civil word
to my lady's gentlewoman, the prim, sour-looking
vestal in the chariot.

I had no more of his company for the rest of
the morning.   He was swept off in the vortex

that followed in the wake of this lady. Once indeed he paused for a moment, as he was hurrying on some errand of the good lady's, to let me know that this was Lady Lillycraft, a sister of the squire's, of large fortune, which the captain would inherit, and that her estate lay in one of the best sporting counties in all England.

FAMILY SERVANTS.

Verily old servants are the vouchers of worthy housekeeping. They are like
rats in a mansion, or mites in a cheese, bespeaking the antiquity and
fatness of their abode.

In my casual anecdotes of the Hall, I may often
be tempted to dwell on circumstances of a trite
and ordinary nature, from their appearing to me
illustrative of genuine national character. It
seems to be the study of the squire to adhere, as
much as possible, to what he considers the old
landmarks of English manners. His servants all
understand his ways, and, for the most part, have
been accustomed to them from infancy; so that,
upon the whole, his household presents one of the
few tolerable specimens that can now be met with,
of the establishment of an English country gentle-

man of the old school. By the by, the servants
are not the least characteristic part of the household; the housekeeper, for instance, has been born
and brought up at the Hall, and has never been
twenty miles from it; yet she has a stately air
that would not disgrace a lady that had figured
at the court of Queen Elizabeth.

I am half-inclined to think that she has caught
it from living so much among the old family
pictures. It may, however, be owing to a consciousness of her importance in the sphere in which she
has always moved; for she is greatly respected in
the neighbouring village, and among the farmers'
wives, and has high authority in the household,
ruling over the servants with quiet but undisputed
sway.

She is a thin old lady, with blue eyes, and
pointed nose and chin. Her dress is always the
same as to fashion. She wears a small, well
starched ruff, a laced stomacher, full petticoats,
and a gown festooned and open in front, which,
on particular occasions, is of ancient silk, the
legacy of some former dame of the family, or an
inheritance from her mother, who was housekeeper
before her. I have a reverence for these old

garments, as I make no doubt they have figured about these apartments in days long past, when they have set off the charms of some peerless family beauty ; and I have sometimes looked from the old housekeeper to the neighbouring portraits, to see whether I could not recognise her antiquated brocade in the dress of some one of those long-waisted dames that smile on me from the walls.

Her hair, which is quite white, is frizzed out in front, and she wears over it a small cap, nicely plaited, and brought down under the chin. Her manners are simple and primitive, heightened a little by a proper dignity of station.

The Hall is her world, and the history of the family the only history she knows, excepting that which she has read in the Bible. She can give a biography of every portrait in the picture gallery, and is a complete family chronicle.

She is treated with great consideration by the squire. Indeed, Master Simon tells me that there is a traditional anecdote current among the servants, of the squire's having been seen kissing her in the picture gallery, when they were both young. As, however, nothing further was ever noticed between them, the circumstance caused no great scandal; only she was observed to take to reading Pamela shortly afterwards, and refused the hand of the village innkeeper, whom she had previously smiled on.

The old butler, who was formerly footman, and a rejected admirer of hers, used to tell the anecdote now and then, at those little cabals that will occasionally take place among the most orderly servants, arising from the common propensity of the governed to talk against administration; but he has left it off, of late years, since he has risen into place, and shakes his head rebukingly when it is mentioned.

It is certain that the old lady will, to this day, dwell on the looks of the squire when he was a young man at college; and she maintains that none of his sons can compare with their father when he was of their age, and was dressed out in his full suit of scarlet, with his hair craped and powdered, and his three-cornered hat.

She has an orphan niece, a pretty, soft-hearted baggage, named Phœbe Wilkins, who has been transplanted to the Hall within a year or two, and been nearly spoiled for any condition of life. She is a kind of attendant and companion of the fair Julia's; and from loitering about the young lady's apartments, reading scraps of novels, and inheriting second-hand finery, has become something between a waiting-maid and a slip-shod fine lady.

She is considered a kind of heiress among the servants, as she will inherit all her aunt's

property; which, if report be true, must be a
round sum of good golden guineas, the accumulated
wealth of two housekeepers' savings; not to
mention the hereditary wardrobe, and the many
little valuables and knick-knacks treasured up in
the housekeeper's room. Indeed the old housekeeper has the reputation among the servants and
the villagers of being passing rich; and there is
a japanned chest of drawers and a large iron-bound
coffer in her room, which are supposed by the
housemaids to hold treasures of wealth.

The old lady is a great friend of Master

Simon, who, indeed, pays a little court to her, as to a person high in authority: and they have many discussions on points of family history, in which, notwithstanding his extensive information, and pride of knowledge, he commonly admits her superior accuracy. He seldom returns to the Hall, after one of his visits to the other branches of the family, without bringing Mrs. Wilkins some remembrance from the ladies of the house where he has been staying.

Indeed all the children in the house look up to the old lady with habitual respect and attachment, and she seems almost to consider them as her own, from their having grown up under her eye. The Oxonian, however, is her favourite, probably from being the youngest, though he is the most mischievous, and has been apt to play tricks upon her from boyhood.

I cannot help mentioning one little ceremony which, I believe, is peculiar to the Hall. After the cloth is removed at dinner, the old housekeeper sails into the room and stands behind the squire's chair, when he fills her a glass of wine with his own hands, in which she drinks the health of the company in a truly respectful yet dignified manner,

and then retires. The squire received the custom
from his father, and has always continued it.

There is a peculiar character about the
servants of old English families that reside principally in the country. They have a quiet, orderly,
respectful mode of doing their duties. They are
always neat in their persons, and appropriately,
and, if I may use the phrase, technically dressed ;
they move about the house without hurry or noise ;
there is nothing of the bustle of employment, or
the voice of command ; nothing of that obtrusive

housewifery that amounts to a torment. You are not persecuted by the process of making you comfortable; yet everything is done, and is done well. The work of the house is performed as if by magic, but it is the magic of system. Nothing is done by fits and starts, nor at awkward seasons; the whole goes on like well-oiled clockwork, where there is no noise nor jarring in its operations.

English servants, in general, are not treated with great indulgence, nor rewarded by many commendations; for the English are laconic and reserved towards their domestics; but an approving nod and kind word from master or mistress, goes as far here, as an excess of praise or indulgence elsewhere. Neither do servants exhibit any animated marks of affection to their employers; yet, though quiet, they are strong in their attachments; and the reciprocal regard of masters or servants, though not ardently expressed, is powerful and lasting in old English families.

The title of "an old family servant" carries with it a thousand kind associations in all parts of the world; and there is no claim upon the home-bred charities of the heart more irresistible than that of having been "born in the house." It is common to see grey-headed domestics of this kind attached to an English family of the "old school," who continue in it to the day of their death in the enjoyment of steady unaffected kindness, and the performance of faithful unofficious duty. I think such instances of attachment speak well for master and servant, and the frequency of them speaks well for national character.

These observations, however, hold good only with families of the description I have mentioned, and with such as are somewhat retired, and pass the greater part of their time in the country. As to the powdered menials that throng the walls of fashionable town residences, they equally reflect the character of the establishments to which they belong; and I know no more complete epitomes of dissolute heartlessness and pampered inutility.

But the good "old family servant!"—The one who has always been linked, in idea, with the home of our heart; who has led us to school in the days of prattling childhood; who has been the confidant of our boyish cares, and schemes, and enterprises; who has hailed us as we came home at vacations, and been the promoter of all our holiday sports; who, when we, in wandering manhood, have left the paternal roof, and only return thither at intervals, will welcome us with a joy inferior only to that of our parents ; who, now grown grey and infirm with age, still totters about the house of our fathers in fond and faithful servitude ; who claims us, in a manner, as his own ; and hastens with querulous eagerness to anticipate his fellow domestics in waiting upon us at table ; and who, when we retire at night to the chamber that still goes by our name, will linger about the room to have one more kind look, and one more pleasant word about times that are past —who does not experience towards such a being a feeling of almost filial affection ?

I have met with several instances of epitaphs on the gravestones of such valuable domestics, recorded with the simple truth of natural feeling. I have two before me at this moment ; one copied from a tombstone of a churchyard in Warwick-shire :

" Here lieth the body of Joseph Batte, con-fidential servant to George Birch, Esq. of Hamp-stead Hall. His grateful friend and master caused this inscription to be written in memory of his discretion, fidelity, diligence, and continence.

He died (a bachelor) aged 84, having lived 44 years in the same family."

The other was taken from a tombstone in Eltham churchyard :

" Here lie the remains of Mr. James Tappy, who departed this life on the 8th of September 1818, aged 84, after a faithful service of 60 years in one family ; by each individual of which he lived respected, and died lamented by the sole survivor."

Few monuments, even of the illustrious, have given me the glow about the heart that I felt while copying this honest epitaph in the churchyard of Eltham. I sympathised with this "sole sur-vivor" of a family, mourning over the grave of the faithful follower of his race, who had been, no doubt, a living memento of times and friends that had passed away ; and in considering this record of long and devoted services, I called to mind the touching speech of Old Adam in "As You Like It," when tottering after the youthful son of his ancient master :

> " Master, go on, and I will follow thee
> To the last gasp, with love and loyalty !"

NOTE.—I cannot but mention a tablet which I have seen some-where in the chapel of Windsor Castle, put up by the late King to the memory of a family servant, who had been a faithful attendant of his lamented daughter, the Princess Amelia. George III. possessed much of the strong domestic feeling of the old English country gentleman ; and it is an incident curious in monumental history, and creditable to the human heart,—a monarch erecting a monument in honour of the humble virtues of a menial.

THE WIDOW.

She was so charitable and pitious
She would weep if that she saw a mous
Caught in a trap, if it were dead or bled ;
Of small hounds had she, that she fed
With rost flesh, milke, and wastel bread ;
But sore wept she if any of them were dead,
Or if man smote them with a yard smart.

CHAUCER.

NOTWITHSTANDING the whimsical parade made by
Lady Lillycraft on her arrival, she has none of the

D

petty stateliness that I had imagined; but on the contrary she has a degree of nature, and simple-heartedness, if I may use the phrase, that mingles well with her old-fashioned manners and harmless ostentation. She dresses in rich silks, with long waist; she rouges considerably, and her hair, which is nearly white, is frizzled out, and put up with pins. Her face is pitted with the small-pox, but the delicacy of her features shows that she may once have been beautiful; and she has a very fair and well-shaped hand and arm, of which, if I mistake not, the good lady is still a little vain.

I have had the curiosity to gather a few particulars concerning her. She was a great belle in town betwen thirty and forty years since, and reigned for two seasons with all the insolence of beauty, refusing several excellent offers; when, unfortunately, she was robbed of her charms and her lovers by an attack of the small-pox. She retired immediately into the country, where she some time after inherited an estate, and married a baronet, a former admirer, whose passion had suddenly revived; "having," as he said, "always loved her mind rather than her person."

The baronet did not enjoy her mind and fortune above six months, and had scarcely grown very tired of her, when he broke his neck in a fox-chase and left her free, rich, and disconsolate. She has remained on her estate in the country ever since, and has never shown any desire to return to town, and revisit the scene of her early triumphs and fatal malady. All her favourite recollections, however, revert to that short period of her youthful beauty. She has no idea of town but as it was at that time ; and continually forgets that the place and people must have changed materially in the course of nearly half a century. She will often speak of the toasts of those days as if still reigning ; and, until very recently, used to talk with delight of the royal family, and the beauty of the young princes and princesses. She cannot be brought to think of the present king otherwise than as an elegant young man, rather wild, but who danced a minuet divinely ; and before he came to the crown, would often mention him as the "sweet young prince."

She talks also of the walks in Kensington Gardens, where the gentlemen appeared in gold-laced coats and cocked hats, and the ladies in

hoops, and swept so proudly along the grassy
avenues; and she thinks the ladies let themselves
sadly down in their dignity, when they gave up
cushioned head-dresses and high-heeled shoes.
She has much to say too of the officers who were
in the train of her admirers; and speaks familiarly
of many wild young blades, that are now, perhaps,
hobbling about watering-places with crutches and
gouty shoes.

Whether the taste the good lady had of matrimony discouraged her or not, I cannot say ; but, though her merits and her riches have attracted many suitors, she has never been tempted to venture again into the happy state. This is singular too, for she seems of a most soft and susceptible heart : is always talking of love and connubial felicity ; and is a great stickler for old-fashioned gallantry, devoted attentions, and eternal constancy, on the part of the gentlemen. She lives, however, after her own taste. Her house, I am told, must have been built and furnished about the time of Sir Charles Grandison : everything about it is somewhat formal and stately ; but has been softened down into a degree of voluptuousness, characteristic of an old lady very tender-hearted and romantic, and that loves her ease. The cushions of the great arm-chairs, and wide sofas, almost bury you when you sit down on them. Flowers of the most rare and delicate kind are placed about the rooms and on little japanned stands ; and sweet bags lie about the tables and mantelpieces. The house is full of pet dogs, Angola cats, and singing birds, who are as carefully waited upon as she is herself.

She is dainty in her living, and a little of an epicure, living on white meats, and little lady-like dishes, though her servants have substantial old English fare, as their looks bear witness. Indeed, they are so indulged, that they are all spoiled, and when they lose their present place they will be fit for no other. Her ladyship is one of those easy-tempered beings that are always doomed to be much liked, but ill served, by their domestics, and cheated by all the world.

Much of her time is passed in reading novels, of which she has a most extensive library, and has a constant supply from the publishers in town. Her erudition in this line of literature is immense : she has kept pace with the press for half a century. Her mind is stuffed with love-tales of all kinds, from the stately amours of the old books of Chivalry, down to the last blue-covered romance, reeking from the press : though she evidently gives the preference to those that came out in the days of her youth, and when she was first in love. She maintains that there are no novels written now-a-days equal to Pamela and Sir Charles Grandison ; and she places the Castle of Otranto at the head of all romances.

She does a vast deal of good in her neighbourhood, and is imposed upon by every beggar in
the county.   She is the benefactress of a village
adjoining to her estate, and takes a special interest in all its love affairs.   She knows of every

courtship that is going on ; every love-lorn damsel
is sure to find a patient listener and sage adviser
in her ladyship.   She takes great pains to recon-
cile all love quarrels, and should any faithless swain
persist in his inconstancy, he is sure to draw on
himself the good lady's violent indignation.

I have learned these particulars partly from
Frank Bracebridge and partly from Master Simon.
I am now able to account for the assiduous
attention of the latter to her ladyship. Her
house is one of his favourite resorts, where he is
a very important personage. He makes her a

visit of business once a year, when he looks
into all her affairs; which, as she is no manager,
are apt to get into confusion. He examines the
books of the overseer, and shoots about the estate,
which, he says, is well stocked with game, not-

withstanding that it is poached by all the vagabonds in the neighbourhood.

It is thought, as I before hinted, that the
captain will inherit the greater part of her property,
having always been her chief favourite ; for, in
fact, she is partial to a red coat. She has now
come to the Hall to be present at his nuptials,
having a great disposition to interest herself in
all matters of love and matrimony.

THE LOVERS.

To a man who is a little of a philosopher, and a bachelor to boot; and who, by dint of some experience in the follies of life, begins to look with a learned eye upon the ways of man, and eke of woman; to such a man, I say, there is something very entertaining in noticing the conduct of a pair of young lovers. It may not be as grave and scientific a study as the loves of the plants, but it is certainly as interesting.

I have therefore derived much pleasure, since my arrival at the Hall, from observing the fair

"The fair Julia was leaning on her lover's arm, listening to his conversation."—PAGE 43.

Julia and her lover. She has all the delightful blushing consciousness of an artless girl, inexperienced in coquetry, who has made her first conquest; while the captain regards her with that mixture of fondness and exultation, with which a youthful lover is apt to contemplate so beauteous a prize.

I observed them yesterday in the garden, advancing along one of the retired walks. The sun was shining with delicious warmth, making great masses of bright verdure, and deep blue shade The cuckoo, that "harbinger of spring," was faintly heard from a distance; the thrush piped from the hawthorn, and the yellow butterflies sported, and toyed, and coquetted in the air.

The fair Julia was leaning on her lover's arm, listening to his conversation, with her eyes cast down, a soft blush on her cheek, and a quiet smile on her lips, while in the hand that hung negligently by her side was a bunch of flowers. In this way they were sauntering slowly along, and when I considered them, and the scene in which they were moving, I could not but think it a thousand pities that the season should ever change, or that young people should ever grow older, or that blossoms should give way to fruit, or that lovers should ever get married.

From what I have gathered of family anecdote, I understand that the fair Julia is the daughter of a favourite college friend of the squire ; who, after leaving Oxford, had entered the army, and served for many years in India, where he was mortally wounded in a skirmish with the natives. In his last moments he had, with a faltering pen, recommended his wife and daughter to the kindness of his early friend.

The widow and her child returned to England helpless, and almost hopeless. When Mr. Bracebridge received accounts of their situation, he hastened to their relief. He reached them just in time to soothe the last moments of the mother, who was dying of a consumption, and to make her happy in the assurance that her child should never want a protector.

The good squire returned with his prattling charge to his stronghold, where he has brought her up with a tenderness truly paternal. As he has taken some pains to superintend her education, and form her taste, she has grown up with many of his notions, and considers him the wisest as

well as the best of men.   Much of her time, too,
has been passed with Lady Lillycraft, who has
instructed her in the manners of the old school,
and enriched her mind with all kinds of novels
and romances.   Indeed, her ladyship has had a
great hand in promoting the match between Julia
and the captain, having had them together at her
country seat the moment she found there was an
attachment growing up between them ; the good
lady being never so happy as when she has a pair
of turtles cooing about her.

I have been pleased to see the fondness with
which the fair Julia is regarded by the old servants
of the Hall.   She has been a pet with them from
childhood, and every one seems to lay some claim
to her education ; so that it is no wonder that she
should be extremely accomplished.   The gardener
taught her to rear flowers, of which she is extremely fond.   Old Christy, the pragmatical huntsman, softens when she approaches ; and as she
sits lightly and gracefully in her saddle, claims the
merit of having taught her to ride ; while the
housekeeper, who almost looks upon her as a
daughter, intimates that she first gave her an
insight into the mysteries of the toilet, having

been dressing-maid in her young days to the late Mrs. Bracebridge. I am inclined to credit this last claim, as I have noticed that the dress of the young lady had an air of the old school, though managed with native taste, and that her hair was put up very much in the style of Sir Peter Lely's portraits in the picture-gallery.

Her very musical attainments partake of this old-fashioned character, and most of her songs are such as are not at the present day to be found on the piano of a modern performer. I have, however, seen so much of modern fashions, modern accomplishments, and modern fine ladies, that I relish this tinge of antiquated style in so young and lovely a girl; and I have had as much pleasure in hearing her warble one of the old songs of Herrick, or Carew, or Suckling, adapted to some simple old melody, as I have had from listening to a lady amateur skylark it up and down through the finest bravura of Rossini or Mozart.

We have very pretty music in the evenings, occasionally, between her and the captain, assisted sometimes by Master Simon, who scrapes, dubiously, on his violin; being very apt to get out, and to halt a note or two in the rear. Sometimes he even thrums a little on the piano, and takes a part in a trio, in which his voice can generally be distinguished by a certain quavering tone, and an occasional false note.

I was praising the fair Julia's performance to him after one of her songs, when I found he took to himself the whole credit of having formed her musical taste, assuring me that she was very apt; and, indeed, summing up her whole character in his knowing way, by adding, that "she was a very nice girl, and had no nonsense about her."

FAMILY RELIQUES.

My Infelice's face, her brow, her eye,
The dimple on her cheek ; and such sweet skill
Hath from the cunning workman's pencil flown,
These lips look fresh and lovely as her own.
False colours last after the true be dead.
Of all the roses grafted on her cheeks,
Of all the graces dancing in her eyes,
Of all the music set upon her tongue,
Of all that was past woman's excellence
In her white bosom ; look, a painted board,
Circumscribes all !   DEKKER.

AN old English family mansion is a fertile subject

for study. It abounds with illustrations of former times, and traces of the tastes, and humours, and manners of successive generations. The alterations and additions, in different styles of architecture; the furniture, plate, pictures, hangings; the warlike and sporting implements of different ages and fancies; all furnish food for curious and amusing speculation. As the squire is very careful in collecting and preserving all family reliques, the Hall is full of remembrances of this kind. In looking about the establishment, I can picture to myself the characters and habits that have prevailed at different eras of the family history. I have mentioned on a former occasion the armour of the crusader which hangs up in the Hall. There are also several jack-boots, with enormously thick soles and high heels, that belonged to a set of cavaliers, who filled the Hall with the din and stir of arms during the time of the Covenanters. A number of enormous drinking vessels of antique fashion, with huge Venice glasses, and green hock glasses, with the apostles in relief on them, remain as monuments of a generation or two of hard-livers, that led a life of roaring revelry, and first introduced the gout into the family.

E

I shall pass over several more such indications of temporary tastes of the squire's predecessors; but I cannot forbear to notice a pair of antlers in the great hall, which is one of the trophies of a hard-riding squire of former times, who was the Nimrod of these parts. There are many traditions of his wonderful feats in hunting still existing, which are related by old Christy, the huntsman, who gets exceedingly nettled if they are in the least doubted. Indeed, there is a frightful chasm, a few miles from the Hall, which goes by the name of the Squire's Leap, from his having cleared it in the ardour of the chase; there can be no doubt of the fact, for old Christy shows the very dints of the horse's hoofs on the rocks on each side of the chasm.

Master Simon holds the memory of this squire in great veneration, and has a number of extraordinary stories to tell concerning him, which he repeats at all hunting dinners; and I am told that they wax more and more marvellous the older they grow. He has also a pair of Ripon spurs which belonged to this mighty hunter of yore, and which he only wears on particular occasions.

The place, however, which abounds most

with mementoes of past times, is the picture-
gallery; and there is something strangely pleasing,
though melancholy, in considering the long rows
of portraits which compose the greater part of the
collection. They furnish a kind of narrative of
the lives of the family worthies, which I am
enabled to read with the assistance of the venerable housekeeper, who is the family chronicler,
prompted occasionally by Master Simon. There
is the progress of a fine lady, for instance, through
a variety of portraits. One represents her as a
little girl, with a long waist and hoop, holding a
kitten in her arms, and ogling the spectator out
of the corners of her eyes, as if she could not turn
her head. In another we find her in the freshness
of youthful beauty, when she was a celebrated
belle, and so hard-hearted as to cause several
unfortunate gentlemen to run desperate and write
bad poetry. In another she is depicted as a
stately dame, in the maturity of her charms; next
to the portrait of her husband, a gallant colonel in
full-bottomed wig and gold-laced hat, who was
killed abroad; and, finally, her monument is
in the church, the spire of which may be seen
from the window, where her effigy is carved in

marble, and represents her as a venerable dame of seventy-six.

In like manner I have followed some of the family great men, through a series of pictures, from early boyhood to the robe of dignity, or truncheon of command, and so on by degrees until they were gathered up in the common repository, the neighbouring church.

There is one group that particularly interested

me. It consisted of four sisters of nearly the same age, who flourished about a century since, and, if I may judge from their portraits, were extremely beautiful. I can imagine what a scene of gaiety and romance this old mansion must have been, when they were in the heyday of their charms; when they passed like beautiful visions through its halls, or stepped daintily to music in the revels and dances of the cedar gallery; or printed, with delicate feet, the velvet verdure of these lawns. How must they have been looked up to with mingled love, and pride, and reverence, by the old family servants; and followed by almost painful admiration by the aching eyes of rival admirers! How must melody, and song, and tender serenade, have breathed about these courts, and their echoes whispered to the loitering tread of lovers! How must these very turrets have made the hearts of the young galliards thrill as they first discerned them from afar, rising from among the trees, and pictured to themselves the beauties casketed like gems within these walls! Indeed I have discovered about the place several faint records of this reign of love and romance, when the Hall was a kind of Court of Beauty. Several of the old romances in the library have marginal notes expressing sympathy and approbation, where there are long speeches extolling ladies' charms, or protesting eternal fidelity, or bewailing the cruelty of some tyrannical fair one.　The interviews, and declarations, and parting scenes of tender lovers, also bear the marks of having been frequently read, and are scored, and marked with notes of admiration, and have initials written on the margins; most of which annotations have the day of the month and year annexed to them.　Several of the windows, too, have scraps of poetry engraved on them with diamonds, taken from the writings of the fair Mrs. Phillips, the once celebrated Orinda.　Some of these seem to have been inscribed by lovers : and others, in a delicate and unsteady hand, and a little inaccurate in the spelling, have evidently been written by the young ladies themselves, or by female friends, who had been on visits to the Hall. Mrs. Phillips seems to have been their favourite author, and they have distributed the names of her heroes and heroines among their circle of intimacy.　Sometimes, in a male hand, the verse bewails the cruelty of beauty and the sufferings of constant love ; while in a female hand it prudishly confines itself to lamenting the parting of female friends. The bow-window of my bedroom, which has, doubtless, been inhabited by one of these beauties, has several of these inscriptions. I have one at this moment before my eyes, called " Camilla parting with Leonora :"

> " How perished is the joy that's past,
>   The present how unsteady !
> What comfort can be great, and last,
>   When this is gone already ! "

And close by it is another, written, perhaps, by some adventurous lover, who had stolen into the lady's chamber during her absence.

> " THEODOSIUS TO CAMILLA.
>
> I'd rather in your favour live,
>   Than in a lasting name ;
> And much a greater rate would give
>   For happiness than fame.
>   THEODOSIUS. 1700."

When I look at these faint records of gallantry and tenderness; when I contemplate the fading portraits of these beautiful girls, and think, too, that they have long since bloomed, reigned, grown old, died, and passed away, and with them all their graces, their triumphs, their rivalries, their admirers; the whole empire of love and pleasure in which they ruled—" all dead, all buried, all forgotten," I find a cloud of melancholy stealing over the present gaieties around me. I was gazing, in a musing mood, this very morning, at the portrait of the lady whose husband was killed abroad, when

the fair Julia entered the gallery, leaning on the arm of the captain. The sun shone through the row of windows on her as she passed along, and she seemed to beam out each time into brightness, and relapse into shade, until the door at the bottom of the gallery closed after her. I felt a sadness of heart at the idea, that this was an emblem of her lot : a few more years of sunshine and shade, and all this life, and loveliness, and enjoyment, will have ceased, and nothing be left to commemorate this beautiful being but one more perishable portrait; to awaken, perhaps, the trite speculations of some future loiterer, like myself, when I and my scribblings shall have lived through our brief existence, and been forgotten.

AN OLD SOLDIER.

I've worn some leather out. abroad ; let out a heathen soul or two ; fed
this good sword with the black blood of pagan Christians ; converted a
few individuals with it. —But let that pass.

THE ORDINARY.

THE Hall was thrown into some little agitation,
a few days since, by the arrival of General
Harbottle. He had been expected for several
days, and had been looked for rather impatiently
by several of the family. Master Simon assured
me that I would like the general hugely, for he
was a blade of the old school, and an excellent
table companion. Lady Lillycraft, also, appeared

to be somewhat fluttered, on the morning of the general's arrival, for he had been one of her early admirers ; and she recollected him only as a dashing young ensign, just come upon the town. She actually spent an hour longer at her toilet, and made her appearance with her hair uncommonly frizzled and powdered, and an additional quantity of rouge. She was evidently a little surprised and shocked, therefore, at finding the little dashing ensign transformed into a corpulent old general, with a double chin, though it was a perfect picture to witness their salutations ; the graciousness of her profound curtsy, and the air of the old school with which the general took off his hat, swayed it gently in his hand, and bowed his powdered head.

All this bustle and anticipation has caused me to study the general with a little more attention than, perhaps, I should otherwise have done ; and the few days that he has already passed at the Hall have enabled me, I think, to furnish a tolerable likeness of him to the reader.

He is, as Master Simon observed, a soldier of the old school, with powdered head, side locks, and pigtail. His face is shaped like the stern of a Dutch man-of-war, narrow at top, and wide at bottom, with full rosy cheeks and a double chin ; so, that, to use the cant of the day, his organs of eating may be said to be powerfully developed.

The general, though a veteran, has seen very little active service, except the taking of Seringapatam, which forms an era in his history. He wears a large emerald in his bosom, and a diamond on his finger, which he got on that occasion, and whoever is unlucky enough to notice either, is sure to involve himself in the whole history of the siege. To judge from the general's conversation, the taking of Seringapatam is the most important affair that has occurred for the last century.

On the approach of warlike times on the Continent, he was rapidly promoted to get him out of the way of younger officers of merit ; until, having been hoisted to the rank of general, he was quietly laid on the shelf. Since that time his campaigns have been principally confined to watering-places ; where he drinks the waters for a slight touch of the liver which he got in India ; and plays whist with old dowagers, with whom he has flirted in his younger days. Indeed he talks of all the fine women of the last half-century, and, according to hints which he now and then drops, has enjoyed the particular smiles of many of them.

He has seen considerable garrison duty, and can speak of almost every place famous for good quarters, and where the inhabitants give good dinners. He is a diner-out of the first-rate currency, when in town; being invited to one place because he has been seen at another. In the same way he is invited about the country seats, and can describe half the seats in the kingdom, from actual observation; nor is any one better versed in court gossip, and the pedigrees and intermarriages of the nobility.

As the general is an old bachelor and an old beau, and there are several ladies at the Hall, especially his quondam flame Lady Jocelyne, he is put rather upon his gallantry. He commonly passes some time, therefore, at his toilet, and takes the field at a late hour every morning, with his hair dressed out and powdered, and a rose in his button-hole. After he has breakfasted, he walks up and down the terrace in the sunshine, humming an air, and hemming between every stave, carrying

one hand behind his back, and with the other touching his cane to the ground, and then raising it up to his shoulder. Should he, in these morning promenades, meet any of the elder ladies of the family, as he frequently does Lady Lillycraft, his hat is immediately in his hand, and it is enough to remind one of those courtly groups of ladies and gentlemen, in old prints of Windsor Terrace or Kensington Gardens.

He talks frequently about "the service," and is fond of humming the old song,

> " Why, soldiers, why,
>   Should we be melancholy, boys?
>   Why, soldiers, why,
>   Whose business 'tis to die !"

I cannot discover, however, that the general has ever run any great risk of dying, excepting from an apoplexy, or indigestion. He criticises all the battles on the Continent, and discusses the merits of the commanders, but never fails to bring the conversation ultimately to Tippoo Saib and Seringapatam. I am told that the general was a perfect champion at drawing-rooms, parades, and watering-places, during the late war, and was looked to with hope and confidence by many an old lady, when labouring under the terror of Buonaparte's invasion.

He is thoroughly loyal, and attends punctually on levees when in town. He has treasured up many remarkable sayings of the late king, particularly one which the king made to him on a field-day, complimenting him on the excellence of his horse. He extols the whole royal family, but especially the present king, whom he pronounces the most perfect gentleman and best whist-player in Europe. The general swears rather more than is the fashion of the present day; but it was the mode of the old school. He is, however, very strict in religious matters, and a staunch church-man. He repeats the responses very loudly in church, and is emphatical in praying for the king and royal family.

At table his loyalty waxes very fervent with his second bottle, and the song of "God save the King" puts him into a perfect ecstasy. He is amazingly well contented with the present state of things, and apt to get a little impatient at any talk about national ruin and agricultural distress. He says he has travelled about the country as much as any man, and has met with nothing but pro-sperity; and to confess the truth, a great part of his time is spent in visiting from one country-seat to another, and riding about the parks of his friends. "They talk of public distress," said the general this day to me, at dinner, as he smacked a glass of rich burgundy, and cast his eyes about the ample board; "they talk of public distress, but where do we find it, sir? I see none. I see no reason any one has to complain. Take my word for it, sir, this talk about public distress is all humbug!"

THE WIDOW'S RETINUE.

Little dogs and all!—LEAR.

IN giving an account of the arrival of Lady Lillycraft at the Hall, I ought to have mentioned the entertainment which I derived from witnessing the unpacking of her carriage, and the disposing of her retinue. There is something extremely amusing to me in the number of factitious wants, the loads of imaginary conveniences, but real incumbrances, with which the luxurious are apt to burthen themselves. I like to watch the whimsical stir and display about one of these petty progresses. The number of robustious footmen and retainers of all kinds bustling about, with looks of infinite gravity and importance, to do almost nothing. The number of heavy trunks and parcels, and handboxes, belonging to my lady; and the solicitude exhibited about some humble, odd-looking box by my lady's maid; the cushions piled in the carriage to make a soft seat still softer, and to prevent the dreaded possibility of a jolt; the smelling-bottles, the cordials, the baskets of biscuit and fruit; the new publications; all pro- vided to guard against hunger, fatigue, or ennui; the led horses to vary the mode of travelling; and all this preparation and parade to move, perhaps, some very good-for-nothing personage about a little space of earth!

I do not mean to apply the latter part of these observations to Lady Lillycraft, for whose simple kindheartedness I have a very great respect, and who is really a most amiable and worthy being. I cannot refrain, however, from mentioning some of the motley retinue she has brought with her; and which, indeed, bespeak the overflowing kind- ness of her nature, which requires her to be surrounded with objects on which to lavish it.

In the first place, her ladyship has a pampered

coachman, with a red face, and cheeks that hang down like dewlaps. He evidently domineers over her a little with respect to the fat horses; and only drives out when he thinks proper, and when he thinks it will be "good for the cattle."

She has a favourite page to attend upon her person; a handsome boy of about twelve years of age, but a mischievous varlet, very much spoiled, and in a fair way to be good for nothing. He is dressed in green, with a profusion of gold cord and gilt buttons about his clothes. She always has one or two attendants of the kind, who are replaced by others as soon as they grow to fourteen years of age. She has brought two dogs with her also, out of a number of pets which she maintains at home. One is a fat spaniel, called

Zephyr—though heaven defend me from such a zephyr! He is fed out of all shape and comfort; his eyes are nearly strained out of his head; he wheezes with corpulency, and cannot walk without great difficulty. The other is a little, old, grey-muzzled curmudgeon, with an unhappy eye, that kindles like a coal if you only look at him; his nose turns up; his mouth is drawn into wrinkles, so as to show his teeth; in short, he has alto-gether the look of a dog far gone in misanthropy, and totally sick of the world. When he walks, he has his tail curled up so tight that it seems to lift his feet from the ground; and he seldom makes use of more than three legs at a time, keeping the other drawn up as a reserve. This last wretch is called Beauty.

These dogs are full of elegant ailments un-known to vulgar dogs; and are petted and nursed by Lady Lillycraft with the tenderest kindness. They are pampered and fed with delicacies by their fellow-minion, the page; but their stomachs are often weak and out of order, so that they can-not eat; though I have now and then seen the page give them a mischievous pinch, or thwack over the head, when his mistress was not by.

They have cushions for their express use, on which they lie before the fire, and yet are apt to shiver and moan if there is the least draught of air. When any one enters the room, they make a most tyrannical barking, that is absolutely deafening. They are insolent to all the other dogs of the establishment. There is a noble staghound, a great favourite of the squire's, who is a privileged visitor to the parlour; but the moment he makes his appearance, these intruders fly at him with furious rage; and I have admired the sovereign indifference and contempt with which he seems to

look down upon his puny assailants. When her ladyship drives out, these dogs are generally carried with her to take the air; when they look out of each window of the carriage, and bark at all vulgar pedestrian dogs. These dogs are a continual source of misery to the household: as they are always in the way, they every now and then get their toes trod on, and then there is a yelping on their part, and a loud lamentation on the part of their mistress, that fills the room with clamour and confusion.

Lastly, there is her ladyship's waiting-gentle-woman, Mrs. Hannah, a prim, pragmatical old maid; one of the most intolerable and intolerant virgins that ever lived. She has kept her virtue by her until it has turned sour, and now every word and look smacks of verjuice. She is the very opposite to her mistress, for one hates, and the other loves, all mankind. How they first came together I cannot imagine, but they have lived together for many years; and the abigail's temper being tart and encroaching, and her ladyship's easy and yielding, the former has got the complete upper hand, and tyrannises over the good lady in secret.

Lady Lillycraft now and then complains of it, in great confidence, to her friends, but hushes up the subject immediately, if Mrs. Hannah makes her appearance. Indeed, she has been so accustomed to be attended by her, that she thinks she could not do without her; though one great study of her life is to keep Mrs. Hannah in good humour, by little presents and kindnesses.

Master Simon has a most devout abhorrence, mingled with awe, for this ancient spinster. He told me the other day, in a whisper, that she was a cursed brimstone—in fact, he added another epithet, which I would not repeat for the world. I have remarked, however, that he is always extremely civil to her when they meet.

READY-MONEY JACK.

My purse, it is my privy wyfe,
This song I dare both syng and say,
It keepeth men from grievous stryfe
When every man for hymself shall pay.
As I ryde in ryche array
For gold and sylver men wyll me floryshe ;
By thys matter I dare well saye,
Ever gramercy myne owne purse.

BOOK OF HUNTING.

ON the skirts of the neighbouring village there
lives a kind of small potentate, who, for aught I
know, is a representative of one of the most ancient
legitimate lines of the present day ; for the empire

over which he reigns has belonged to his family time out of mind. His territories comprise a considerable number of good fat acres; and his seat of power is an old farm-house, where he enjoys, unmolested, the stout oaken chair of his ancestors. The personage to whom I allude is a sturdy old yeoman of the name of John Tibbets, or rather Ready-Money Jack Tibbets, as he is called throughout the neighbourhood.

The first place where he attracted my attention was in the churchyard on Sunday; where he sat on a tombstone after service, with his hat a little on one side, holding forth to a small circle of auditors, and, as I presumed, expounding the law and the prophets, until, on drawing a little nearer, I found he was only expatiating on the merits of a brown horse. He presented so faithful a picture of a substantial English yeoman, such as he is often described in books, heightened, indeed, by some little finery peculiar to himself, that I could not but take note of his whole appearance.

He was between fifty and sixty, of a strong muscular frame, and at least six feet high, with a physiognomy as grave as a lion's, and set off with short, curling, iron-gray locks. His shirt-collar was turned down, and displayed a neck covered with the same short, curling, gray hair; and he wore a coloured silk neckcloth, tied very loosely, and tucked in at the bosom, with a green paste brooch on the knot. His coat was of dark-green cloth, with silver buttons, on each of which was engraved a stag, with his own name, John Tibbets, underneath. He had an inner waistcoat of figured chintz, between which and his coat was another of scarlet cloth unbuttoned. His breeches were also left unbuttoned at the knees, not from any sloven-liness, but to show a broad pair of scarlet garters. His stockings were blue, with white clocks; he wore large silver shoe-buckles; a broad paste buckle in his hatband; his sleeve buttons were gold seven-shilling pieces; and he had two or three guineas hanging as ornaments to his watch-chain.

On making some inquiries about him, I gathered that he was descended from a line of farmers that had always lived on the same spot, and owned the same property; and that half of the churchyard was taken up with the tombstones of his race. He has all his life been an important character in the place. When a youngster, he was one of the most roaring blades of the neighbourhood. No one could match him at wrestling, pitching the bar, cudgel play, and other athletic exercises. Like the renowned Pinner of Wakefield, he was the village champion ; carried off the prize at all the fairs, and threw his gauntlet at the country round. Even to this day the old people talk of his prowess, and undervalue, in comparison, all heroes of the green that have succeeded him ; nay, they say that if Ready-Money Jack were to take the field even now, there is no one could stand before him.

When Jack's father died, the neighbours shook their heads, and predicted that young Hopeful would soon make way with the old homestead ; but Jack falsified all their predictions. The moment he succeeded to the paternal farm he assumed a new character ; took a wife ; attended resolutely to his affairs, and became an industrious, thrifty farmer. With the family property he inherited a set of old family maxims, to which he steadily adhered. He saw to everything himself ; put his own hand to the plough ; worked hard ; ate heartily ; slept soundly ; paid for everything in cash down ; and never danced except he could do it to the music of his own money in both pockets. He has never been without a hundred

or two pounds in gold by him, and never allows a
debt to stand unpaid. This has gained him his
current name, of which, by the by, he is a little
proud ; and has caused him to be looked upon as
a very wealthy man by all the village.

Notwithstanding his thrift, however, he has
never denied himself the amusements of life, but
has taken a share in every passing pleasure. It
is his maxim, that " he that works hard can afford
to play." He is, therefore, an attendant at all the
country fairs and wakes, and has signalised himself
by feats of strength and prowess on every village
green in the shire. He often makes his appearance at horse-races, and sports his half-guinea and
even his guinea at a time ; keeps a good horse
for his own riding, and to this day is fond of following the hounds, and is generally in at the death.

He keeps up the rustic revels, and hospitalities too, for which his paternal farm-house has always been noted; has plenty of good cheer and dancing at harvest-home, and above all, keeps the "merry night,"* as it is termed, at Christmas.

With all his love of amusement, however, Jack is by no means a boisterous jovial companion. He is seldom known to laugh even in the midst of his gaiety; but maintains the same grave, lion-like demeanour. He is very slow at comprehending a joke; and is apt to sit puzzling at it, with a perplexed look, while the rest of the company is in a roar. This gravity has, perhaps, grown on him with the growing weight of his character; for he is gradually rising into patriarchal dignity in his native place. Though he no longer takes an active part in athletic sports, yet he always presides at them, and is appealed to on all occasions as umpire. He maintains the peace on the village-green at holiday games, and quells all

---

* MERRY NIGHT; a rustic merry-making in a farm-house about Christmas, common in some parts of Yorkshire. There is abundance of homely fare, tea, cakes, fruit, and ale; various feats of agility, amusing games, romping, dancing, and kissing withal. They commonly break up at midnight.

brawls and quarrels by collaring the parties and
shaking them heartily, if refractory.   No one ever
pretends to raise a hand against him, or to contend
against his decisions; the young men having
grown up in habitual awe of his prowess, and in
implicit deference to him as the champion and
lord of the green.

He is a regular frequenter of the village inn,
the landlady having been a sweetheart of his in
early life, and he having always continued on kind
terms with her.   He seldom, however, drinks
anything but a draught of ale; smokes his pipe,

and pays his reckoning before leaving the tap-
room. Here he "gives his little senate laws;"
decides bets, which are very generally referred to
him; determines upon the characters and qualities
of horses; and indeed plays now and then the
part of a judge, in settling petty disputes between
neighbours, which otherwise might have been
nursed by country attorneys into tolerable law-
suits. Jack is very candid and impartial in his
decisions, but he has not a head to carry a long
argument, and is very apt to get perplexed and
out of patience if there is much pleading. He
generally breaks through the argument with a
strong voice, and brings matters to a summary
conclusion, by pronouncing what he calls the
"upshot of the business," or, in other words, "the
long and short of the matter."

Jack once made a journey to London, a great
many years since, which has furnished him with
topics of conversation ever since. He saw the
old king on the terrace at Windsor, who stopped,
and pointed him out to one of the princesses, being
probably struck with Jack's truly yeoman-like
appearance. This is a favourite anecdote with
him, and has no doubt had a great effect in

making him a most loyal subject ever since, in
spite of taxes and poor's rates. He was also
at Bartholomew-fair, where he had half the
buttons cut off his coat; and a gang of pick-
pockets, attracted by his external show of gold
and silver, made a regular attempt to hustle him
as he was gazing at a show; but for once they
found that they had caught a tartar, for Jack
enacted as great wonders among the gang as
Samson did among the Philistines. One of his
neighbours, who had accompanied him to town,
and was with him at the fair, brought back an
account of his exploits, which raised the pride of
the whole village; who considered their champion
as having subdued all London, and eclipsed the
achievements of Friar Tuck, or even the renowned
Robin Hood himself.

Of late years the old fellow has begun to take
the world easily; he works less, and indulges in
greater leisure, his son having grown up, and
succeeded to him both in the labours of the farm
and the exploits of the green. Like all sons of
distinguished men, however, his father's renown is
a disadvantage to him, for he can never come up
to public expectation. Though a fine, active

fellow of three-and-twenty, and quite the "cock of the walk," yet the old people declare he is nothing like what Ready-Money Jack was at his time of life.   The youngster himself acknowledges his inferiority, and has a wonderful opinion of the old man, who indeed taught him all his athletic accomplishments, and holds such a sway over him, that I am told, even to this day, he would have no hesitation to take him in hands, if he rebelled against paternal government.

The squire holds Jack in very high esteem, and shows him to all his visitors as a specimen of old English "heart of oak."   He frequently calls at his house, and tastes some of his home-brewed, which is excellent.   He made Jack a present of old Tusser's Hundred Points of good Husbandrie, which has furnished him with reading ever since, and is his text-book and manual in all agricultural and domestic concerns.   He has made dog's ears at the most favourite passages, and knows many of the poetical maxims by heart.

Tibbets, though not a man to be daunted or fluttered by high acquaintances; and though he cherishes a sturdy independence of mind and manner, yet is evidently gratified by the attentions of the squire, whom he has known from boyhood, and pronounces "a true gentleman every inch of him." He is also on excellent terms with Master Simon, who is a kind of privy councillor to the family; but his great favourite is the Oxonian, whom he taught to wrestle and play at quarter-staff when a boy, and considers the most promising young gentleman in the whole county.

BACHELORS.

The Bachelor most joyfully
  In pleasant plight doth pass his daies,
Good fellowship and companie
  He doth maintain and kepe alwaies.

EVANS' OLD BALLADS.

THERE is no character in the comedy of human life that is more difficult to play well than that of an old bachelor. When a single gentleman, therefore, arrives at that critical period when he begins to consider it an impertinent question to be asked his age, I would advise him to look well to his ways. This period, it is true, is much later with some men than with others; I have witnessed more than once the meeting of two wrinkled old lads of this kind, who had not seen each other for several years, and have been amused by the amicable exchange of compliments on each other's appearance that takes place on such occasions. There is always one invariable observation, " Why, bless my soul! you look younger than when last I saw you!" Whenever a man's friends begin to compliment him about looking young, he may be sure that they think he is growing old.

I am led to make these remarks by the conduct of Master Simon and the general, who have become great cronies. As the former is the younger by many years, he is regarded as quite a youthful gallant by the general, who moreover looks upon him as a man of great wit and prodigious acquirements. I have already hinted that Master Simon is a family beau, and considered rather a young fellow by all the elderly ladies of the connexion; for an old bachelor, in an old family connexion, is something like an actor in a regular dramatic corps, who seems " to flourish in immortal youth," and will continue to play the Romeos and Rangers for half a century together.

Master Simon, too, is a little of the chameleon, and takes a different hue with every different companion : he is very attentive and officious, and somewhat sentimental, with Lady Lillycraft ; copies out little namby-pamby ditties and love-songs for her, and draws quivers, and doves, and darts, and Cupids, to be worked in the corners of her pocket handkerchiefs. He indulges, however, in very considerable latitude with the other married ladies of the family ; and has many sly pleasantries to whisper to them, that provoke an equivocal laugh and tap of the fan. But when he gets among young company, such as Frank Bracebridge, the Oxonian, and the general, he is apt to put on the mad wig, and to talk in a very bachelor-like strain about the sex.

In this he has been encouraged by the example of the general, whom he looks up to as a man who has seen the world. The general, in fact, tells shocking stories after dinner, when the ladies have retired, which he gives as some of the choice things that are served up at the Mulligatawney Club, a knot of boon companions in London. He also repeats the fat jokes of old Major Pendergast, the wit of the club, and which, though the general can hardly repeat them for laughing, always make Mr. Bracebridge look grave, he having a great

"I saw him and Master Simon conversing with a buxom milkmaid in a meadow."—PAGE 87.

antipathy to an indecent jest. In a word, the
general is a complete instance of the declension in
gay life, by which a young man of pleasure is apt
to cool down into an obscene old gentleman.

I saw him and Master Simon, an evening or
two since, conversing with a buxom milkmaid in a
meadow ; and from their elbowing each other now
and then, and the general's shaking his shoulders,
blowing up his cheeks, and breaking out into a
short fit of irrepressible laughter, I had no doubt
they were playing the mischief with the girl.

As I looked at them through a hedge, I could
not but think they would have made a tolerable
group for a modern picture of Susannah and the
two elders. It is true the girl seemed in no wise
alarmed at the force of the enemy ; and I question,
had either of them been alone, whether she would
not have been more than they would have
ventured to encounter. Such veteran roisters
are daring wags when together, and will put any
female to the blush with their jokes ; but they are
as quiet as lambs when they fall singly into the
clutches of a fine woman.

In spite of the general's years, he evidently is
a little vain of his person, and ambitious of con-

quests. I have observed him on Sunday in church
eyeing the country girls most suspiciously; and
have seen him leer upon them with a downright
amorous look, even when he has been gallanting
Lady Lillycraft with great ceremony through the
churchyard. The general, in fact, is a veteran in
the service of Cupid rather than of Mars, having
signalised himself in all the garrison towns and
country quarters, and seen service in every ball-
room of England. Not a celebrated beauty but
he has laid siege to; and if his words may be
taken in a matter wherein no man is apt to be
over veracious, it is incredible what success he
has had with the fair. At present he is like a
worn-out warrior, retired from service; but who
still cocks his beaver with a military air, and talks
stoutly of fighting whenever he comes within the
smell of gunpowder.

I have heard him speak his mind very freely
over his bottle, about the folly of the captain in
taking a wife; as he thinks a young soldier should
care for nothing but his "bottle and kind landlady." But, in fact, he says, the service on the
continent has had a sad effect upon the young
men; they have been ruined by light wines and

French quadrilles. " They've nothing," he says, " of the spirit of the old service. There are none of your six-bottle men left, that were the souls of a mess-dinner, and used to play the very deuce among the women."

As to a bachelor, the general affirms that he is a free and easy man, with no baggage to take care of but his portmanteau ; but, as Major Pendergast says, a married man, with his wife hanging on his arm, always puts him in mind of a chamber candlestick, with its extinguisher hitched to it. I should not mind all this if it were merely confined to the general; but I fear he will be the ruin of my friend, Master Simon, who already begins to echo his heresies, and to talk in the style of a gentleman that has seen life, and lived upon the town. Indeed, the general seems to have taken Master Simon in hand, and talks of showing him the lions when he comes to town, and of introducing him to a knot of choice spirits at the Mulligatawney Club ; which, I understand, is composed of old nabobs, officers in the Company's employ, and other "men of Ind," that have seen service in the East, and returned home burnt out with curry and touched with the liver complaint. They have

their regular club, where they eat Mulligatawney
soup, smoke the hookah, talk about Tippoo Saib,
Seringapatam, and tiger-hunting ; and are tediously
agreeable in each other's company.

A Literary Antiquary.

Printed bookes he contemnes, as a novelty of this latter age ; but a manuscript he pores on everlastingly ; especially if the cover be all moth-
eaten, and the dust make a parenthesis between every syllable.

Mico-Cosmographie, 1628.

THE squire receives great sympathy and support
in his antiquated humours, from the parson, of
whom I made some mention on my former visit
to the Hall, and who acts as a kind of family chap-
lain.   He has been cherished by the squire almost
constantly since the time that they were fellow-
students at Oxford ; for it is one of the peculiar
advantages of these great universities, that they
often link the poor scholar to the rich patron, by
early and heartfelt ties, that last through life,

without the usual humiliations of dependence and patronage. Under the fostering protection of the squire, therefore, the little parson has pursued his studies in peace. Having lived almost entirely among books, and those, too, old books, he is quite ignorant of the world, and his mind is as antiquated as the garden at the Hall, where the flowers are all arranged in formal beds, and the yew-trees clipped into urns and peacocks.

His taste for literary antiquities was first imbibed in the Bodleian Library at Oxford; where, when a student, he passed many an hour foraging among the old manuscripts. He has since, at different times, visited most of the curious libraries in England, and has ransacked many of the cathedrals. With all his quaint and curious learning, he has nothing of arrogance or pedantry; but that unaffected earnestness and guileless simplicity which seem to belong to the literary antiquary.

He is a dark, mouldy little man, and rather dry in his manner : yet, on his favourite theme, he kindles up, and at times is even eloquent. No fox-hunter, recounting his last day's sport, could be more animated than I have seen the worthy

parson, when relating his search after a curious
document, which he had traced from library to
library, until he fairly unearthed it in the dusty
chapter-house of a cathedral. When, too, he
describes some venerable manuscript, with its rich
illuminations, its thick creamy vellum, its glossy
ink, and the odour of the cloisters that seemed to
exhale from it, he rivals the enthusiasm of a
Parisian epicure, expatiating on the merits of a
Perigord pie, or a *Pâté de Strasbourg.*

His brain seems absolutely haunted with love-
sick dreams about gorgeous old works in "silk
linings, triple gold bands, and tinted leather,
locked up in wire cases, and secured from the
vulgar hands of the mere reader;" and, to continue
the happy expression of an ingenious writer,
"dazzling one's eyes, like eastern beauties peering
through their jealousies."

He has a great desire, however, to read such
works in the old libraries and chapter-houses to
which they belong; for he thinks a black-letter
volume reads best in one of those venerable
chambers where the light struggles through dusty
lancet windows and painted glass; and that it
loses half its zest if taken away from the neigh-

bourhood of the quaintly carved oaken book-case and Gothic reading-desk. At his suggestion, the squire has had the library furnished in this antique taste, and several of the windows glazed with painted glass, that they may throw a properly tempered light upon the pages of their favourite old authors.

The parson, I am told, has been for some time meditating a commentary on Strutt, Brand, and Douce, in which he means to detect them in sundry dangerous errors in respect to popular games and superstitions; a work to which the squire looks forward with great interest. He is also a casual contributor to that long-established repository of national customs and antiquities, the Gentleman's Magazine, and is one of those that every now and then make an inquiry concerning some obsolete customs or rare legend; nay, it is said that several of his communications have been at least six inches in length. He frequently receives parcels by coach from different parts of the kingdom, containing mouldy volumes and almost illegible manuscripts; for it is singular what an active correspondence is kept up among literary antiquaries, and how soon the fame of any rare volume, or unique copy, just discovered among the rubbish of a library, is circulated among them. The parson is more busy than common just now, being a little flurried by an advertisement of a work, said to be preparing for the press, on the mythology of the middle ages. The little man has long been gathering together all the hobgoblin tales he could collect, illustrative of the superstitions of former times; and he is in a complete fever lest this formidable rival should take the field before him.

Shortly after my arrival at the Hall, I called at the parsonage, in company with Mr. Bracebridge and the general. The parson had not been seen for several days, which was a matter of some surprise, as he was an almost daily visitor at the Hall. We found him in his study, a small, dusky chamber, lighted by a lattice window that looked into the churchyard, and was overshadowed by a yew-tree. His chair was surrounded by folios and quartos, piled upon the floor, and his table was covered with books and manuscripts. The cause of his seclusion was a work which he had recently received, and with which he had retired in rapture from the world, and shut himself up to

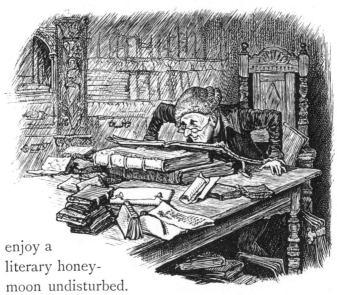

enjoy a
literary honey-
moon undisturbed.
Never did boarding-school girl devour the pages
of a sentimental novel, or Don Quixote a chivalrous
romance, with more intense delight than did the
little man banquet on the pages of this delicious
work. It was Dibdin's Bibliographical Tour; a
work calculated to have as intoxicating an effect
on the imaginations of literary antiquaries, as the
adventures of the heroes of the Round Table on
all true knights; or the tales of the early American
voyagers on the ardent spirits of the age, filling

them with dreams of Mexican and Peruvian mines, and of the golden realm of El Dorado.

The good parson had looked forward to this bibliographical expedition as of far greater importance than those to Africa, or the North Pole. With what eagerness had he seized upon the history of the enterprise! With what interest had he followed the redoubtable bibliographer and his graphical squire in their adventurous roamings among Norman castles and cathedrals, and French libraries, and German convents and universities; penetrating into the prison-houses of vellum manuscripts and exquisitely illuminated missals, and revealing their beauties to the world!

When the parson had finished a rapturous eulogy on this most curious and entertaining work, he drew forth from a little drawer a manuscript lately received from a correspondent, which perplexed him sadly. It was written in Norman-French in very ancient characters, and so faded and mouldered away as to be almost illegible. It was apparently an old Norman drinking song, that might have been brought over by one of William the Conqueror's carousing followers. The writing was just legible enough to keep a

H

keen antiquity hunter on a doubtful chase; here and there he would be completely thrown out, and then there would be a few words so plainly written as to put him on the scent again. In this way he had been led on for a whole day, until he had found himself completely at fault.

The squire endeavoured to assist him, but was equally baffled. The old general listened for some time to the discussion, and then asked the parson if he had read Captain Morris's or George Stephens's or Anacreon Moore's bacchanalian songs; on the other replying in the negative, "Oh, then," said the general, with a sagacious nod, "if you want a drinking song, I can furnish you with the latest collection—I did not know you had a turn for those kind of things; and I can lend you the Encyclopædia of Wit into the bargain. I never travel without them; they're excellent reading at an inn."

It would not be easy to describe the odd look of surprise and perplexity of the parson at this proposal; or the difficulty the squire had in making the general comprehend, that though a jovial song of the present day was but a foolish sound in the ears of wisdom, and beneath the notice of a learned man, yet a trowl written by a tosspot several hundred years since was a matter worthy of the gravest research, and enough to set whole colleges by the ears.

I have since pondered much on this matter, and have figured to myself what may be the fate of our current literature, when retrieved piecemeal by future antiquaries, from among the rubbish of ages. What a Magnus Apollo, for instance, will Moore become among sober divines and dusty schoolmen! Even his festive and amatory songs, which are now the mere quickeners of our social moments, or the delights of our drawing-rooms, will then become matters of laborious research and painful collation. How many a grave professor will then waste his midnight oil, or worry his brain through a long morning, endeavouring to restore the pure text, or illustrate the biographical hints of "Come tell me, says Rosa, as kissing and kissed;" and how many an arid old book-worm, like the worthy little parson, will give up in despair, after vainly striving to fill up some fatal hiatus in "Fanny of Timmol!"

Nor is it merely such exquisite authors as Moore that are doomed to consume the oil of future antiquaries.   Many a poor scribbler, who is now apparently sent to oblivion by pastry-cooks and cheesemongers, will then rise again in fragments, and flourish in learned immortality.

After all, thought I, time is not such an invariable destroyer as he is represented.   If he pulls down, he likewise builds up ; if he impoverishes one, he enriches another; his very dilapidations furnish matter for new works of controversy, and his rust is more precious than the most costly gilding.   Under his plastic hand trifles rise into importance ; the nonsense of one age becomes the wisdom of another ; the levity of the wit gravitates into the learning of the pedant, and an ancient farthing moulders into infinitely more value than a modern guinea.

—— Love and hay
Are thick sown, but come up full of thistles.
BEAUMONT AND FLETCHER.

I WAS so much pleased with the anecdotes which were told me of Ready-Money Jack Tibbets, that I got Master Simon, a day or two since, to take me to his house. It was an old-fashioned farm-house, built of brick, with curiously twisted chimneys. It stood at a little distance from the road, with a southern exposure, looking upon a soft green slope of meadow. There was a small garden in front, with a row of beehives humming among beds of sweet herbs and flowers. Well-scoured milking tubs, with bright copper hoops, hung on the garden paling. Fruit trees were trained up against the cottage, and pots of flowers stood in the windows. A fat superannuated mastiff lay in the sunshine at the door; with a sleek cat sleeping peacefully across him.

Mr. Tibbets was from home at the time of our calling, but we were received with hearty and homely welcome by his wife—a notable, motherly woman, and a complete pattern for wives, since, according to Master Simon's account, she never contradicts honest Jack, and yet manages to have her own way, and to control him in everything. She received us in the main room of the house, a kind of parlour or hall, with great brown beams of timber across it, which Mr. Tibbets is apt to point out with some exultation, observing that they don't put such timber in houses now-a-days. The furniture was old-fashioned, strong, and highly polished; the walls were hung with coloured prints of the story of the Prodigal Son, who was represented in a red coat and leather breeches. Over the fireplace was a blunderbuss, and a hard-favoured likeness of Ready-Money Jack, taken, when he was a young man, by the same artist that painted the tavern sign; his mother having taken a notion that the Tibbetses had as much right to have a gallery of family portraits as the folks at the Hall.

The good dame pressed us very much to take some refreshment, and tempted us with a variety of household dainties, so that we were glad to compound by tasting some of her home-made wines. While we were there, the son and heir-apparent came home; a good-looking young fellow, and something of a rustic beau. He took us over the premises, and showed us the whole establishment. An air of homely but substantial plenty prevailed throughout; everything was of the best materials, and in the best condition. Nothing was out of place, or ill made; and you saw everywhere the signs of a man that took care to have the worth of his money, and that paid as he went.

The farm-yard was well stocked; under a shed was a taxed cart, in trim order, in which Ready-Money Jack took his wife about the country. His well-fed horse neighed from the stable, and when led out into the yard, to use the words of

young Jack, "he shone like a bottle;" for he said
the old man made it a rule that everything about
him should fare as well as he did himself.

I was pleased to see the pride which the young
fellow seemed to have of his father.   He gave us
several particulars concerning his habits, which
were pretty much to the effect of those I have
already mentioned.   He had never suffered an
account to stand in his life, always providing the
money before he purchased anything; and, if
possible, paying in gold and silver.   He had a
great dislike to paper money, and seldom went
without a considerable sum in gold about him.   On
my observing that it was a wonder he had never

been waylaid and robbed, the young fellow smiled
at the idea of any one venturing upon such an ex-
ploit, for I believe he thinks the old man would
be a match for Robin Hood and all his gang.

I have noticed that Master Simon seldom goes
into any house without having a world of private
talk with some one or other of the family, being a
kind of universal counsellor and confidant. We
had not been long at the farm before the old
dame got him into a corner of her parlour, where
they had a long whispering conference together;
in which I saw by his shrugs that there were some
dubious matters discussed, and by his nods that he
agreed with everything she said.

After we had come out, the young man accompanied us a little distance, and then, drawing
Master Simon aside into a green lane, they
walked and talked together for nearly half-an-hour.
Master Simon, who has the usual propensity of
confidants to blab everything to the next friend
they meet with, let me know that there was a love
affair in question; the young fellow having been
smitten with the charms of Phœbe Wilkins, the
pretty niece of the housekeeper at the Hall.
Like most other love concerns, it had brought

its troubles and perplexities. Dame Tibbets had long been on intimate gossiping terms with the housekeeper, who often visited the farm-house; but when the neighbours spoke to her of the likelihood of a match between her son and Phœbe Wilkins, " Marry come up !" she scouted the very idea. The girl had acted as lady's maid, and it was beneath the blood of the Tibbetses, who had lived on their own lands time out of mind, and owed reverence and thanks to nobody, to have the heir-apparent marry a servant !

These vapourings had faithfully been carried to the housekeeper's ear by one of the mutual go-between friends. The old housekeeper's blood, if not as ancient, was as quick as that of Dame Tibbets.

She had been accustomed to carry a high head at the Hall and among the villagers; and her faded brocade rustled with indignation at the slight cast upon her alliance by the wife of a petty farmer. She maintained that her niece had been a companion rather than a waiting-maid to the young ladies. " Thank heavens, she was not obliged to work for her living, and was as idle as any young lady in the land; and when somebody died, would receive something that would be worth the notice of some folks with all their ready money."

A bitter feud had thus taken place between the two worthy dames, and the young people were forbidden to think of one another. As to young Jack, he was too much in love to reason upon the matter; and being a little heady, and not standing in much awe of his mother, was ready to sacrifice the whole dignity of the Tibbetses to his passion. He had lately, however, had a violent quarrel with his mistress, in consequence of some coquetry on her part, and at present stood aloof. The politic mother was exerting all her ingenuity to widen this accidental breach; but, as is most commonly the case, the more she meddled with this perverse inclination of her son, the stronger it grew. In the meantime Old Ready-Money was kept completely in the dark; both parties were in awe and uncertainty as to what might be his way of taking the matter, and dreaded to awaken the sleeping lion. Between father and son, therefore, the worthy Mrs. Tibbets was full of business and at her wits' end. It is true that there was no great danger of honest Ready-Money's finding the thing out, if left to himself; for he was of a most unsuspicious temper, and by no means quick of apprehension; but there was daily risk of his attention being aroused by those cobwebs which his indefatigable wife was continually spinning about his nose.

Such is the distracted state of politics in the domestic empire of Ready-Money Jack; which only shows the intrigues and internal dangers to which the best regulated governments are liable. In this perplexing situation of their affairs, both mother and son have applied to Master Simon for counsel; and, with all his experience in meddling with other people's concerns, he finds it an exceedingly difficult part to play, to agree with both parties, seeing that their opinions and wishes are so diametrically opposite.

HORSEMANSHIP.

A coach was a strange monster in those days, and the sight of one put both horse and man into amazement. Some said it was a great crabshell brought out of China, and some imagined it to be one of the Pagan temples in which the Cannibals adored the divell.

TAYLOR, THE WATER POET.

I HAVE made casual mention, more than once, of one of the squire's antiquated retainers, old Christy the huntsman. I find that his crabbed humour is a source of much entertainment among the young men of the family: the Oxonian, particularly, takes a mischievous pleasure now and then in slyly rubbing the old man against the grain, and then smoothing him down again; for the old fellow is as ready to bristle up his back as a porcupine. He rides a venerable hunter called Pepper, which is a counterpart of himself, a heady, cross-grained animal, that frets the flesh off its bones; bites, kicks, and plays all manner of villanous tricks. He is as tough, and nearly as old as his rider, who has ridden him time out of mind, and is, indeed, the only one that can do anything with him. Sometimes, however, they have a complete quarrel, and a dispute for mastery, and then, I am told, it is as good as a farce to see the heat they both get into, and the wrongheaded contest that ensues; for they are quite knowing in each other's ways and in the art of teasing and fretting each other. Notwithstanding these doughty brawls, however, there is nothing that nettles old Christy sooner than to question the merits of his horse; which he upholds as tenaciously as a faithful husband will vindicate the virtues of the termagant spouse that gives him a curtain lecture every night of his life.

The young men call old Christy their "professor of equitation," and in accounting for the appellation, they let me into some particulars of the squire's mode of bringing up his children.

There is an odd mixture of eccentricity and good sense in all the opinions of my worthy host. His mind is like modern Gothic, where plain brickwork is set off with pointed arches and plain tracery. Though the main groundwork of his opinions is correct, yet he has a thousand little notions, picked up from old books, which stand out whimsically on the surface of his mind.

Thus, in educating his boys, he chose Peachum, Markham, and such old English writers for his manuals. At an early age he took the lads out of their mother's hands, who was disposed, as mothers are apt to be, to make fine orderly children of them, that should keep out of sun and rain, and never soil their hands, nor tear their clothes.

In place of this, the squire turned them loose, to run free and wild about the park, without heeding wind or weather. He was also particularly attentive in making them bold and expert horsemen; and these were the days when old Christy, the huntsman, enjoyed great importance, as the lads were put under his care to practise them at the leaping-bars, and to keep an eye upon them in the chase.

The squire always objected to their using

carriages of any kind, and is still a little tenacious on this point. He often rails against the universal use of carriages, and quotes the words of honest Nashe to that effect. " It was thought," says Nashe, in his Quaternio, " a kind of solecism, and to savour of effeminacy, for a young gentleman in the flourishing time of his age to creep into a coach, and to shroud himself from wind and weather : our great delight was to out-brave the blustering boreas upon a great horse; to arm and prepare ourselves to go with Mars and Bellona into the field was our sport and pastime ; coaches and caroches we left unto them for whom they were first invented, for ladies and gentlemen, and decrepit age and impotent people."

The squire insists that the English gentlemen have lost much of their hardiness and manhood since the introduction of carriages. "Compare," he will say, "the fine gentleman of former times, ever on horseback, booted and spurred, and travel-stained, but open, frank, manly, and chivalrous, with the fine gentleman of the present day, full of affectation and effeminacy, rolling along a turnpike in his voluptuous vehicle. The young men of those days were rendered brave, and lofty, and

generous, in their notions, by almost living in
their saddles, and having their foaming steeds
'like proud seas under them.' There is something," he adds, "in bestriding a fine horse, that
makes a man feel more than mortal. He seems
to have doubled his nature, and to have added
to his own courage and sagacity the power, the
speed, and stateliness of the superb animal on
which he is mounted."

"It is a great delight," says old Nashe, "to
see a young gentleman with his skill and cunning,
by his voice, rod, and spur, better to manage and

I

to command the great Bucephalus, than the strongest Milo, with all his strength; one while to see him make him tread, trot, and gallop the ring; and one after to see him make him gather up roundly; to bear his head steadily; to run a full career swiftly; to stop a sudden lightly; anon after to see him make him advance, to yorke, to go back and side long, to turn on either hand; to gallop the gallop galliard; to do the capriole, the chambetta, and dance the curvetty."

In conformity to these ideas, the squire had them all on horseback at an early age, and made them ride, slap-dash, about the country, without flinching at hedge or ditch, or stone wall, to the imminent danger of their necks.

Even the fair Julia was partially included in this system; and, under the instructions of old Christy, has become one of the best horsewomen in the county. The squire says it is better than all the cosmetics and sweeteners of the breath that ever were invented. He extols the horsemanship of the ladies in former times, when Queen Elizabeth would scarcely suffer the rain to stop her accustomed ride. "And then think," he will say, "what nobler and sweeter beings it made them. What a difference must there be, both in mind and body, between a joyous high-spirited dame of those days, glowing with health and exercise, freshened by every breeze that blows, seated loftily and gracefully on her saddle, with plume on head, and hawk on hand, and her descendant of the present day, the pale victim of routs and ball-rooms, sunk languidly in one corner of an enervating carriage."

The squire's equestrian system has been attended with great success, for his sons, having passed through the whole course of instruction without breaking neck or limb, are now healthful, spirited, and active, and have the true Englishman's love for a horse. If their manliness and frankness are praised in their father's hearing, he quotes the old Persian maxim, and says, they have been taught " to ride, to shoot, and to speak the truth."

It is true the Oxonian has now and then practised the old gentleman's doctrines a little in the extreme. He is a gay youngster, rather fonder of his horse than his book, with a little dash of the dandy; though the ladies all declare that he is "the flower of the flock." The first year that he was sent to Oxford, he had a tutor appointed to overlook him, a dry chip of the university. When he returned home in the vacation, the squire made many inquiries about how he liked his college, his studies, and his tutor. "Oh, as to my tutor, sir, I have parted with him some time since." "You have; and, pray, why so?" "Oh, sir, hunting was all the go at our college, and I was a little short of funds; so I discharged my tutor, and took a horse, you know." "Ah, I was not aware of that, Tom," said the squire, mildly.

When Tom returned to college his allowance was doubled, that he might be enabled to keep both horse and tutor.

LOVE SYMPTOMS.

I will now begin to sigh, read poets, look pale, go neatly, and be most apparently in love. Marston.

I SHOULD not be surprised if we should have another pair of turtles at the Hall, for Master Simon has informed me, in great confidence, that he suspects the general of some design upon the susceptible heart of Lady Lillycraft. I have, indeed, noticed a growing attention and courtesy in the veteran towards her ladyship; he softens very much in her company, sits by her at table, and entertains her with long stories about Serin-

gapatam, and pleasant anecdotes of the Mulligatawney Club. I have even seen him present her
with a full-blown rose from the hot-house, in a style
of the most captivating gallantry, and it was accepted with great suavity and graciousness; for
her ladyship delights in receiving the homage and
attention of the sex.

Indeed, the general was one of the earliest
admirers that dangled in her train during her
short reign of beauty; and they flirted together
for half a season in London, some thirty or forty
years since. She reminded him lately, in the
course of conversation about former days, of the
time when he used to ride a white horse, and to
canter so gallantly by the side of her carriage in
Hyde Park; whereupon I have remarked that the
veteran has regularly escorted her since, when she
rides out on horseback; and I suspect he almost
persuades himself that he makes as captivating an
appearance as in his youthful days.

It would be an interesting and memorable
circumstance in the chronicles of Cupid, if this
spark of the tender passion, after lying dormant
for such a length of time, should again be fanned
into a flame from amidst the ashes of two burnt-

out hearts. It would be an instance of perdurable fidelity, worthy of being placed beside those recorded in one of the squire's favourite tomes, commemorating the constancy of the olden times; in which times, we are told, "men and wymmen coulde love togyders seven yeres, and no licours luste swere betwene them, and thenne was love, trouthe, and feythfulness; and lo in lyke wyse was used love in Kyng Arthurs dayes."*

Still, however, this may be nothing but a little venerable flirtation, the general being a veteran dangler, and the good lady habituated to these kind of attentions. Master Simon, on the other hand, thinks the general is looking about him with the wary eye of an old campaigner; and now that he is on the wane, is desirous of getting into warm winter quarters.

Much allowance, however, must be made for Master Simon's uneasiness on the subject, for he looks on Lady Lillycraft's house as one of the strongholds where he is lord of the ascendant; and, with all his admiration of the general, I much doubt whether he would like to see him lord of the lady and the establishment.

* Mort d'Arthur.

There are certain other symptoms, notwithstanding, that give an air of probability to Master Simon's intimations. Thus, for instance, I have observed that the general has been very assiduous in his attentions to her ladyship's dogs, and has several times exposed his fingers to imminent jeopardy in attempting to pat Beauty on the head. It is to be hoped his advances to the mistress will be more favourably received, as all his overtures towards a caress are greeted by the pestilent little cur with a wary kindling of the eye, and a most

venomous growl. He has, moreover, been very complaisant towards the lady's gentlewoman, the immaculate Mrs. Hannah, whom he used to speak of in a way that I do not choose to mention. Whether she has the same suspicions with Master Simon or not, I cannot say; but she receives his civilities with no better grace than the implacable Beauty; unscrewing her mouth into a most acid smile, and looking as though she could bite a piece out of him. In short, the poor general seems to have as formidable foes to contend with as a hero of ancient fairy tale, who had to fight his way to his enchanted princess through ferocious monsters of every kind, and to encounter the brimstone terrors of some fiery dragon.

There is still another circumstance which inclines me to give very considerable credit to Master Simon's suspicions. Lady Lillycraft is very fond of quoting poetry, and the conversation often turns upon it, on which occasions the general is thrown completely out. It happened the other day that Spenser's Fairy Queen was the theme for the great part of the morning, and the poor general sat perfectly silent. I found him not long after in the library with spectacles on nose, a book in his hand, and fast asleep. On my approach he awoke, slipped the spectacles into his pocket, and began to read very attentively. After a little while he put a paper in the place, and laid the volume aside, which I perceived was the Fairy Queen. I have had the curiosity to watch how he got on in his poetical studies; but though I have repeatedly seen him with the book in his hand, yet I find the paper has not advanced above three or four pages; the general being extremely apt to fall asleep when he reads.

FALCONRY.

Ne is there hawk which mantleth on her perch,
　　Whether high tow'ring or accousting low,
But I the measure of her flight doe search,
　　And all her prey and all her diet know.　　SPENSER.

THERE are several grand sources of lamentation
furnished to the worthy squire, by the improve-
ment of society, and the grievous advancement of
knowledge; among which there is none, I believe,
that causes him more frequent regret than the
unfortunate invention of gunpowder.　To this he
continually traces the decay of some favourite
custom, and, indeed, the general downfall of all
chivalrous and romantic usages.　"English soldiers,"
he says, "have never been the men they were in the

days of the cross-bow and the long-bow; when they depended upon the strength of the arm, and the English archer could draw a cloth-yard shaft to the head. These were the times when, at the battles of Cressy, Poictiers, and Agincourt, the French chivalry was completely destroyed by the bowmen of England. The yeomanry, too, have never been what they were, when, in times of peace, they were constantly exercised with the bow, and archery was a favourite holiday pastime."

Among the other evils which have followed in the train of this fatal invention of gunpowder, the squire classes the total decline of the noble art of falconry. "Shooting," he says, "is a skulking, treacherous, solitary sport in comparison; but hawking was a gallant, open, sunshiny recreation; it was the generous sport of hunting carried into the skies."

"It was, moreover," he says, "according to Braithewaite, the stately amusement of high and mounting spirits; for, as the old Welsh proverb affirms, in those times 'You might know a gentleman by his hawk, horse, and greyhound.' Indeed, a cavalier was seldom seen abroad without his hawk on his fist; and even a lady of rank did not

think herself completely equipped, in riding forth,
unless she had her tassel-gentel held by jesses on
her delicate hand. It was thought in those excellent days, according to an old writer, 'quite
sufficient for noblemen to winde their horn, and
to carry their hawke fair; and leave study and
learning to the children of mean people.'"

Knowing the good squire's hobby, therefore, I
have not been surprised at finding that, among
the various recreations of former times which he
has endeavoured to revive in the little world in
which he rules, he has bestowed great attention
on the noble art of falconry. In this he of course
has been seconded by his indefatigable coadjutor,
Master Simon : and even the parson has thrown
considerable light on their labours, by various
hints on the subject, which he has met with in old
English works. As to the precious work of that
famous dame, Julianna Barnes; the Gentleman's
Academie, by Markham; and the other well-
known treatises that were the manuals of ancient
sportsmen, they have them at their fingers' ends :
but they have more especially studied some old
tapestry in the house, whereon is represented a
party of cavaliers and stately dames, with doublets,

caps, and flaunting feathers, mounted on horse, with attendants on foot, all in animated pursuit of the game.

The squire has discountenanced the killing of any hawks in his neighbourhood, but gives a liberal bounty for all that are brought him alive; so that the Hall is well stocked with all kinds of birds of prey. On these he and Master Simon have exhausted their patience and ingenuity, endeavouring to "reclaim" them, as it is termed, and to train them up for the sport; but they have met with continual checks and disappointments. Their feathered school has turned out the most intractable and graceless scholars; nor is it the least of their trouble to drill the retainers who were to act as ushers under them, and to take immediate charge of these refractory birds. Old Christy and the gamekeeper both, for a time, set their faces against the whole plan of education; Christy having been nettled at hearing what he terms a wild-goose chase put on a par with a fox-hunt; and the gamekeeper having always been accustomed to look upon hawks as arrant poachers, which it was his duty to shoot down, and nail, *in terrorem*, against the out-houses.

Christy has at length taken the matter in hand, but has done still more mischief by his intermeddling. He is as positive and wrongheaded about this as he is about hunting. Master Simon has continual disputes with him as to feeding and training the hawks. He reads to him long passages from the old authors I have mentioned; but Christy, who cannot read, has a sovereign contempt for all book-knowledge, and persists in treating the hawks according to his

own notions, which are drawn from his experience, in younger days, in rearing of game cocks.

The consequence is, that, between these jarring systems, the poor birds have had a most trying and unhappy time of it. Many have fallen victims to Christy's feeding and Master Simon's physicking; for the latter has gone to work *secundum artem*, and has given them all the vomitings and scourings laid down in the books; never were poor hawks so fed and physicked before. Others have been lost by being but half 'reclaimed,' or tamed; for on being taken into the field, they have 'raked,' after the game quite out of hearing of the call, and never returned to school.

All these disappointments had been petty, yet sore grievances to the squire, and had made him to despond about success. He has lately, however, been made happy by the receipt of a fine Welsh falcon, which Master Simon terms a stately highflyer. It is a present from the squire's friend, Sir Watkyn Williams Wynn; and is, no doubt, a descendant of some ancient line of Welsh princes of the air, that have long lorded it over their kingdom of clouds, from Wynnstay to the very summit of Snowdon, or the brow of

Penmanmawr. Ever since the squire received this invaluable present, he has been as impatient to sally forth and make proof of it, as was Don Quixote to assay his suit of armour. There have been some demurs as to whether the bird was in proper health and training; but these have been overruled by the vehement desire to play with a new toy; and it has been determined, right or wrong, in season or out of season, to have a day's sport in hawking to-morrow.

The Hall, as usual, whenever the squire is about to make some new sally on his hobby, is all agog with the thing. Miss Templeton, who is brought up in reverence for all her guardian's humours, has proposed to be of the party, and Lady Lillycraft has talked also of riding out to the scene of action and looking on. This has gratified the old gentleman extremely; he hails it as an auspicious omen of the revival of falconry, and does not despair but the time will come when it will be again the pride of a fine lady to carry about a noble falcon in preference to a parrot or a lapdog.

I have amused myself with the bustling preparations of that busy spirit, Master Simon, and

K

the continual thwartings he receives from that genuine son of a pepper-box, old Christy. They have had half a dozen consultations about how the hawk is to be prepared for the morning's sport. Old Nimrod, as usual, has always got in a pet, upon which Master Simon has invariably given up the point, observing in a good-humoured tone, "Well, well, have it your own way, Christy; only don't put yourself in a passion;" a reply which always nettles the old man ten times more than ever.

HAWKING.

The soaring hawk, from fist that flies,
   Her falconer doth constrain
Sometimes to range the ground about
   To find her out again ;
And if by sight, or sound of bell,
   His falcon he may see,
Wo ho ! he cries, with cheerful voice—
   The gladdest man is he.

Handefull of pleasant delites.

At an early hour this morning the Hall was in a bustle, preparing for the sport of the day. I heard Master Simon whistling and singing under my window at sunrise, as he was preparing the jesses for the hawk's legs, and could distinguish now and then a stanza of one of his favourite old ditties :

> " In peascod time, when hound to horn
> Gives note that buck be kill'd ;
> And little boy with pipe of corn
> Is tending sheep a-field," etc.

A hearty breakfast, well flanked by cold meats, was served up in the great hall. The whole garrison of retainers and hangers-on were in motion, reinforced by volunteer idlers from the village. The horses were led up and down before the door; everybody had something to say and something to do, and hurried hither and thither; there was a direful yelping of dogs; some that were to accompany us being eager to set off, and others that were to stay at home being whipped back to their kennels. In short, for once, the good squire's mansion might have been taken as a good specimen of one of the rantipole establishments of the good old feudal times.

Breakfast being finished, the chivalry of the Hall prepared to take the field. The fair Julia was of the party, in a hunting-dress, with a light plume of feathers in her riding-hat. As she mounted her favourite Galloway, I remarked, with pleasure, that old Christy forgot his usual crustiness, and hastened to adjust her saddle and bridle. He touched his cap as she smiled on him and thanked him; and then, looking round at the other attendants, gave a knowing nod of his head, in which I read pride and exultation at the charming appearance of his pupil.

Lady Lillycraft had likewise determined to witness the sport. She was dressed in her broad white beaver, tied under the chin, and a riding-habit of the last century. She rode her sleek, ambling pony, whose motion was as easy as a rocking-chair; and was gallantly escorted by the general, who looked not unlike one of the doughty heroes in the old prints of the battle of Blenheim. The parson, likewise, accompanied her on the other side; for this was a learned amusement in which he took great interest; and, indeed, had given much counsel, from his knowledge of old customs.

At length everything was arranged, and off we set from the Hall. The exercise on horseback puts one in fine spirits; and the scene was gay and animating. The young men of the family accompanied Miss Templeton. She sat lightly and gracefully in her saddle, her plumes dancing and waving in the air; and the group had a charming effect as they appeared and disappeared among the trees, cantering along with the bounding animation of youth. The squire and Master Simon rode together, accompanied by old Christy mounted on Pepper. The latter bore the hawk on his fist, as he insisted the bird was most accustomed to him. There was a rabble rout on foot, composed of retainers from the Hall, and some idlers from the village, with two or three spaniels for the purpose of starting the game.

A kind of corps de reserve came on quietly in the rear, composed of Lady Lillycraft, General Harbottle, the parson, and a fat footman. Her ladyship ambled gently along on her pony, while the general, mounted on a tall hunter, looked down upon her with an air of the most protecting gallantry.

For my part, being no sportsman, I kept with this last party, or rather lagged behind, that I might take in the whole picture; and the parson occasionally slackened his pace and jogged on in company with me.

The sport led us at some distance from the Hall, in a soft meadow reeking with the moist verdure of spring. A little river ran through it, bordered by willows, which had put forth their tender early foliage. The sportsmen were in quest of herons, which were said to keep about this stream.

There was some disputing already among the leaders of the sport. The squire, Master Simon, and old Christy, came every now and then to a pause, to consult together, like the field officers in an army; and I saw, by certain motions of the head, that Christy was as positive as any old wrong-headed German commander.

As we were prancing up this quiet meadow every sound we made was answered by a distinct echo, from the sunny wall of an old building, that lay on the opposite margin of the stream; and I paused to listen to the "spirit of a sound," which seems to love such quiet and beautiful places. The parson informed me that this was the ruin of an ancient grange, and was supposed by the country people to be haunted by a dobbie, a kind of rural sprite, something like Robin-Good-fellow. They often fancied the echo to be the voice of the dobbie answering them, and were rather shy of disturbing it after dark. He added, that the squire was very careful of this ruin, on account of the superstition connected with it. As I considered this local habitation of an " airy nothing," I called to mind the fine description of an echo in Webster's Duchess of Malfy :

> —— " 'Yond side o' th' river lies a wall,
> Piece of a cloister, which in my opinion
> Gives the best echo that you have ever heard :
> So plain in the distinction of our words
> That many have supposed it a spirit
> That answers."

The parson went on to comment on a pleasing and fanciful appellation which the Jews of old gave to the echo, which they called Bath-kool, that is to say, "the daughter of the voice;" they considered it an oracle, supplying in the second temple the want of the Urim and Thummim, with which the first was honoured.* The little man was just entering very largely and learnedly upon the subject, when we were startled by a prodigious bawling, shouting, and yelping. A flight of crows, alarmed by the approach of our forces, had suddenly risen from a meadow; a cry was put up by the rabble rout on foot. " Now, Christy! now is your time, Christy!" The squire and Master Simon, who were beating up the river banks in quest of a heron, called out eagerly to Christy to keep quiet; the old man, vexed and bewildered by the confusion of voices, completely lost his head : in his flurry he slipped off the hood, cast off the falcon, and away flew the crows, and away soared the hawk.

I had paused on a rising ground, close to Lady Lillycraft and her escort, from whence I had

* Bekker's *Monde Enchanté*.

a good view of the sport. I was pleased with the appearance of the party in the meadow, riding along in the direction that the bird flew; their bright beaming faces turned up to the bright skies as they watched the game; the attendants on foot scampering along, looking up, and calling out, and the dogs bounding and yelping with clamorous sympathy.

The hawk had singled out a quarry from among the carrion crew. It was curious to see the efforts of the two birds to get above each other; one to make the fatal swoop, the other to avoid it. Now they crossed athwart a bright feathery cloud, and now they were against the

clear blue sky. I confess, being no sportsman, I
was more interested for the poor bird that was
striving for its life, than for the hawk that was
playing the part of a mercenary soldier. At
length the hawk got the upper hand, and
made a rushing stoop at her quarry, but the
latter made as sudden a surge downwards, and
slanting up again evaded the blow, screaming
and making the best of his way for a dry tree
on the brow of a neighbouring hill; while the
hawk, disappointed of her blow, soared up again
into the air, and appeared to be "raking" off.
It was in vain old Christy called and whistled,
and endeavoured to lure her down; she paid
no regard to him; and, indeed, his calls were
drowned in the shouts and yelps of the
army of militia that had followed him into the
field.

Just then an exclamation from Lady Lillycraft
made me turn my head. I beheld a complete
confusion among the sportsmen in the little vale
below us. They were galloping and running
towards the edge of a bank; and I was shocked
to see Miss Templeton's horse galloping at large
without his rider. I rode to the place to which

the others were hurrying, and when I reached the bank, which almost overhung the stream, I saw at the foot of it the fair Julia, pale, bleeding, and apparently lifeless, supported in the arms of her frantic lover.

In galloping heedlessly along, with her eyes turned upward, she had unwarily approached too near the bank; it had given way with her, and she and her horse had been precipitated to the pebbled margin of the river.

I never saw greater consternation, The captain was distracted; Lady Lillycraft fainting; the squire in dismay; and Master Simon at his wits' end. The beautiful creature at length showed signs of returning life; she opened her eyes; looked around her upon the anxious group, and comprehending in a moment the nature of the scene, gave a sweet smile, and putting her hand in her lover's, exclaimed feebly, " I am not much hurt, Guy!" I could have taken her to my heart for that single exclamation.

It was found, indeed, that she had escaped, almost miraculously, with a contusion of the head, a sprained ankle, and some slight bruises. After her wound was stanched, she was taken to a neighbouring cottage until a carriage could be summoned to convey her home; and when this had arrived, the cavalcade, which had issued forth so gaily on this enterprise, returned slowly and pensively to the Hall.

I had been charmed by the generous spirit shown by this young creature, who, amidst pain and danger, had been anxious only to relieve the distress of those around her. I was gratified, therefore, by the universal concern displayed by the domestics on our return. They came crowding down the avenue, each eager to render assistance. The butler stood ready with some curiously delicate cordial; the old housekeeper was provided with half a dozen nostrums, prepared by her own hands, according to the family receipt book; while her niece, the melting Phœbe, having no other way of assisting, stood wringing her hands and weeping aloud.

The most material effect that is likely to follow this accident is a postponement of the nuptials, which were close at hand. Though I commiserate the impatience of the captain on that account, yet I shall not otherwise be sorry at the delay, as it will give me a better opportunity of studying the characters here assembled, with which I grow more and more entertained.

I cannot but perceive that the worthy squire is quite disconcerted at the unlucky result of his hawking experiment, and this unfortunate illustration of his eulogy on female equitation. Old Christy, too, is very waspish, having been sorely twitted by Master Simon for having let his hawk fly at carrion. As to the falcon, in the confusion occasioned by the fair Julia's disaster the bird was totally forgotten. I make no doubt she has made the best of her way back to the hospitable Hall of Sir Watkyn Williams Wynn ; and may very possibly, at this present writing, be pluming her wings among the breezy bowers of Wynnstay.

FORTUNE-TELLING.

Each city, each town, and every village
Affords us either an alms or pillage.
And if the weather be cold and raw,
Then in a barn we tumble on straw.
If warm and fair, by yea-cock and nay-cock,
The fields will afford us a hedge or a hay-cock.

MERRY BEGGARS.

As I was walking one evening with the Oxonian,
Master Simon, and the general, in a meadow not
far from the village, we heard the sound of a fiddle
rudely played, and looking in the direction from
whence it came, we saw a thread of smoke curling
up from among the trees. The sound of music is

always attractive; for, wherever there is music, there is good humour, or goodwill. We passed along a footpath, and had a peep, through a break in the hedge, at the musician and his party, when the Oxonian gave us a wink, and told us that if we would follow him we should have some sport.

It proved to be a gipsy encampment, consisting of three or four little cabins, or tents, made of blankets and sail-cloth, spread over hoops that were stuck in the ground. It was on one side of a green lane, close under a hawthorn hedge, with a broad beech-tree spreading above it. A small rill tinkled along close by, through the fresh sward, that looked like a carpet.

A tea-kettle was hanging by a crooked piece of iron, over a fire made from dry sticks and leaves, and two old gipsies, in red cloaks, sat crouched on the grass, gossiping over their evening cup of tea; for these creatures, though they live in the open air, have their ideas of fireside comforts. There were two or three children sleeping on the straw with which the tents were littered; a couple of donkeys were grazing in the lane, and a thievish-looking dog was lying before the fire. Some of the younger gipsies were dancing to the music of

L

a fiddle, played by a tall, slender stripling, in an old frock coat, with a peacock's feather stuck in his hatband.

As we approached, a gipsy girl, with a pair of fine roguish eyes, came up, and, as usual, offered  to tell our fortunes. I could not but admire a certain degree of slattern elegance about the baggage. Her long black silken hair was curiously plaited in numerous small braids, and negligently put up in a picturesque style that a painter might have been proud to have devised. Her dress was of a figured chintz, rather ragged, and not over clean, but of a variety of most harmonious and agreeable colours; for these beings have a singularly fine eye for colours. Her straw hat was in her hand, and a red cloak thrown over one arm.

The Oxonian offered at once to have his fortune told, and the girl began with the usual volubility of her race; but he drew her on one side near the hedge, as he said he had no idea of having his secrets overheard. I saw he was talking to her instead of she to him, and by his glancing towards us now and then, that he was giving the baggage some private hints. When they returned to us, he assumed a very serious air. "Zounds!" said he, "it's very astonishing how these creatures come by their knowledge; this girl has told me some things that I thought no one knew but myself!"

The girl now assailed the general: "Come, your honour," said she, "I see by your face you're a lucky man; but you're not happy in your mind; you're not, indeed, sir; but have a good heart, and give me a good piece of silver, and I'll tell you a nice fortune."

The general had received all her approaches with a banter, and had suffered her to get hold of his hand; but at the mention of the piece of silver, he hemmed, looked grave, and turning to us, asked if we had not better continue our walk. "Come, my master," said the girl archly, "you'd not be in such a hurry, if you knew all that I could tell you about a fair lady that has a notion for you. Come, sir, old love burns strong; there's many a one comes to see weddings that go away brides themselves!" Here the girl whispered something in a low voice, at which the general coloured up, was

a little fluttered, and suffered himself to be drawn aside under the hedge, where he appeared to listen to her with great earnestness, and at the end paid her half-a-crown with the air of a man that has got the worth of his money.

The girl next made her attack upon Master

Simon, who, however, was too old a bird to be caught, knowing that it would end in an attack upon his purse, about which he is a little sensitive. As he has a great notion, however, of being considered a roister, he chucked her under the chin, played her off with rather broad jokes, and put on something of the rake-helly air, that we see now and then assumed on the stage by the sad-boy gentlemen of the old school. "Ah, your honour," said the girl, with a malicious leer, "you were not in such a tantrum last year when I told you about the widow you know who; but if you had taken a friend's advice, you'd never have come away from Doncaster races with a flea in your ear!"

There was a secret sting in this speech that seemed quite to disconcert Master Simon. He jerked away his hand in a pet, smacked his whip, whistled to his dogs, and intimated that it was high time to go home. The girl, however, was determined not to lose her harvest. She now turned upon me, and, as I have a weakness of spirit where there is a pretty face concerned, she soon wheedled me out of my money, and in return read me a fortune which, if it prove true, and I am determined to believe it, will make me one of the luckiest men in the chronicles of Cupid.

I saw that the Oxonian was at the bottom of all this oracular mystery, and was disposed to amuse himself with the general, whose tender approaches to the widow have attracted the notice of the wag. I was a little curious, however, to know the meaning of the dark hints which had so suddenly disconcerted Master Simon : and took occasion to fall in the rear with the Oxonian on our way home, when he laughed heartily at my questions, and gave me ample information on the subject.

The truth of the matter is, that Master Simon has met with a sad rebuff since my Christmas visit to the Hall. He used at that time to be joked about a widow, a fine dashing woman, as he privately informed me. I had supposed the pleasure he betrayed on these occasions resulted from the usual fondness of old bachelors for being teased about getting married, and about flirting, and being fickle and false-hearted. I am assured, however, that Master Simon had really persuaded himself the widow had a kindness for him ; in consequence of which he had been at some extraordinary expense in new clothes, and had actually got Frank Bracebridge to order him a coat from Stultz. He began to throw out hints about the importance of a man's settling himself in life before he grew old ; he would look grave whenever the widow and matrimony were mentioned in the same sentence; and privately asked the opinion of the squire and parson about the prudence of marrying a widow with a rich jointure, but who had several children.

An important member of a great family connection cannot harp much upon the theme of matrimony without its taking wind; and it soon got buzzed about that Mr. Simon Bracebridge was actually gone to Doncaster races, with a new horse, but that he meant to return in a curricle with a lady by his side. Master Simon did, indeed, go to the races, and that with a new horse; and the dashing widow did make her appearance in her curricle; but it was unfortunately driven by a strapping young Irish dragoon, with whom even Master Simon's self-complacency would not allow him to enter into competition, and to whom she was married shortly after.

It was a matter of sore chagrin to Master Simon for several months, having never before been fully committed. The dullest head in the

family had a joke upon him; and there is no one
that likes less to be bantered than an absolute
joker. He took refuge for a time at Lady Lillycraft's, until the matter should blow over; and
occupied himself by looking over her accounts,
regulating the village choir, and inculcating loyalty
into a pet bullfinch by teaching him to whistle
"God save the King."

He has now pretty nearly recovered from the
mortification; holds up his head, and laughs as
much as any one; again affects to pity married
men, and is particularly facetious about widows,

when Lady Lillycraft is not by. His only time of trial is when the general gets hold of him, who is infinitely heavy and persevering in his waggery, and will interweave a dull joke through the various topics of a whole dinner-time. Master Simon often parries these attacks by a stanza from his old work of "Cupid's Solicitor for Love :"

> " 'Tis in vain to woo a widow over long,
>   In once or twice her mind you may perceive ;
> Widows are subtle, be they old or young,
>   And by their wiles young men they will deceive."

LOVE-CHARMS.

—— Come, do not weep, my girl,
Forget him, pretty pensiveness ; there will
Come others, every day, as good as he.

Sir J. Suckling.

THE approach of a wedding in a family is always
an event of great importance, but particularly so
in a household like this, in a retired part of the
country. Master Simon, who is a pervading
spirit, and, through means of the butler and

housekeeper, knows everything that goes forward, tells me that the maid-servants are continually trying their fortunes, and that the servants' hall has of late been quite a scene of incantation.

It is amusing to notice how the oddities of the head of a family flow down through all the branches. The squire, in the indulgence of his love of everything that smacks of old times, has held so many grave conversations with the parson at table, about popular superstitions and traditional rites, that they have been carried from the parlour to the kitchen by the listening domestics, and, being apparently sanctioned by such high authorities, the whole house has become infected by them.

The servants are all versed in the common modes of trying luck, and the charms to ensure constancy. They read their fortunes by drawing strokes in the ashes, or by repeating a form of words, and looking in a pail of water. St. Mark's Eve, I am told, was a busy time with them; being an appointed night for certain mystic ceremonies. Several of them sowed hemp-seed, to be reaped by their true lovers; and they even ventured upon the solemn and fearful preparation of the dumb-cake. This must be done fasting and in silence. The ingredients are handed down in traditional form :—" An egg-shell full of salt, an egg-shell full of malt, and an egg-shell full of barley meal." When the cake is ready, it is put upon a pan over the fire, and the future husband will appear, turn the cake, and retire; but if a word is spoken, or a fast is broken, during this awful ceremony, there is no knowing what horrible consequence would ensue!

The experiments in the present instance came to no result; they that sowed the hemp-seed forgot the magic rhyme that they were to pronounce, so the true lover never appeared ; and as to the dumb-cake, what between the awful stillness they had to keep, and the awfulness of the midnight hour, their hearts failed them when they had put the cake in the pan, so that, on the striking of the great house-clock in the servants' hall, they were seized with a sudden panic, and ran out of the room, to which they did not return until morning, when they found the mystic cake burnt to a cinder.

The most persevering at these spells, however,

is Phœbe Wilkins, the housekeeper's niece. As she is a kind of privileged personage, and rather idle, she has more time to occupy herself with these matters. She has always had her head full of love and matrimony, she knows the dreaming book by heart, and is quite an oracle among the little girls of the family, who always come to her to interpret their dreams in the mornings.

During the present gaiety of the house, however, the poor girl has worn a face full of trouble; and, to use the housekeeper's words, " has fallen into a sad hystericky way lately." It seems that she was born and brought up in the village, where her father was parish-clerk, and she was an early playmate and sweetheart of young Jack Tibbets. Since she has come to live at the Hall, however, her head has been a little turned. Being very pretty, and naturally genteel, she has been much noticed and indulged: and being the house-keeper's niece, she has held an equivocal station between a servant and a companion. She has learnt something of fashions and notions among the young ladies, which have effected quite a metamorphosis; insomuch that her finery at church on Sundays has given mortal offence to her former intimates in the village. This has occasioned the misrepresentations which have awakened the implacable family pride of Dame Tibbets. But what is worse, Phœbe, having a spice of coquetry in her disposition, showed it on one or two occasions to her lover, which produced

a downright quarrel; and Jack, being very proud and fiery, has absolutely turned his back upon her for several successive Sundays.

The poor girl is full of sorrow and repentance, and would fain make up with her lover; but he feels his security, and stands aloof. In this he is doubtless encouraged by his mother, who is continually reminding him of what he owes to his family; for this same family pride seems doomed to be the eternal bane of lovers.

As I hate to see a pretty face in trouble, I have felt quite concerned for the luckless Phœbe, ever since I heard her story. It is a sad thing to be thwarted in love at any time, but particularly so at this tender season of the year, when every living thing, even to the very butterfly, is sporting with its mate; and the green fields and the budding groves, and the singing of the birds, and the sweet smell of the flowers, are enough to turn the head of a love-sick girl. I am told that the coolness of Young Ready-Money lies heavy at poor Phœbe's heart. Instead of singing about the house as formerly, she goes about, pale and sighing, and is apt to break into tears when her companions are full of merriment.

Mrs. Hannah, the vestal gentlewoman of my Lady Lillycraft, has had long talks and walks with

Phœbe, up and down the avenue, of an evening; and has endeavoured to squeeze some of her own verjuice into the other's milky nature. She speaks with contempt and abhorrence of the whole sex, and advises Phœbe to despise all the men as heartily as she does. But Phœbe's loving temper is not to be curdled; she has no such thing as hatred or contempt for mankind in her whole composition. She has all the simple fondness of heart of poor, weak, loving woman; and her only thoughts at present are, how to conciliate and reclaim her wayward swain.

The spells and love-charms, which are matters of sport to the other domestics, are serious concerns with this love-stricken damsel. She is continually trying her fortune in a variety of ways. I am told that she has absolutely fasted for six Wednesdays and three Fridays successively, having understood that it was a sovereign charm to ensure being married to one's liking within the year. She carries about, also, a lock of her sweetheart's hair, and a riband he once gave her, being a mode of producing constancy in her lover. She even went so far as to try her fortune by the moon, which has always had much

to do with lovers' dreams and fancies. For this
purpose she went out in the night of the full

moon, knelt on a stone in the meadow, and
repeated the old traditonal rhyme :

> " All hail to thee, moon, all hail to thee :
> I pray thee, good moon, now show to me
> The youth who my future husband shall be."

When she came back to the house, she was
faint and pale, and went immediately to bed.
The next morning she told the porter's wife that

she had seen some one close by the hedge in the meadow, which she was sure was young Tibbets; at any rate, she had dreamt of him all night; both of which, the old dame assured her, were most happy signs. It has since turned out that the person in the meadow was old Christy, the huntsman, who was walking his nightly rounds with the great staghound; so that Phœbe's faith in the charm is completely shaken.

A BACHELOR'S CONFESSIONS.

I'll have a private, pensive single life.
THE COLLIER OF CROYDON.

 I WAS sitting in my room a morning or two since, reading, when some one tapped at the door, and Master Simon entered. He had an unusually fresh appearance; he had put on a bright green riding-coat, with a bunch of violets in the button-hole, and had the air of an old bachelor trying to rejuvenate himself. He had not, however, his usual briskness and vivacity, but loitered about the room with somewhat of absence of manner, humming the old song,—" Go, lovely rose, tell her that wastes her time and me;" and then, leaning against the window, and looking upon the

landscape, he uttered a very audible sigh. As I had not been accustomed to see Master Simon in a pensive mood, I thought there might be some vexation preying on his mind, and I endeavoured to introduce a cheerful strain of conversation ; but he was not in the vein to follow it up, and proposed that we should take a walk.

It was a beautiful morning, of that soft vernal temperature, that seems to thaw all the frost out of one's blood, and to set all nature in a ferment. The very fishes felt its influence : the cautious trout ventured out of his dark hole to seek his mate, the roach and the dace rose up to the surface of the brook to bask in the sunshine, and the amorous frog piped from among the rushes. If ever an oyster can really fall in love, as has been said or sung, it must be on such a morning.

The weather certainly had its effect even upon Master Simon, for he seemed obstinately bent upon the pensive mood. Instead of stepping briskly along, smacking his dog-whip, whistling quaint ditties, or telling sporting anecdotes, he leaned on my arm, and talked about the approaching nuptials ; from whence he made several digressions upon the character of womankind, touched

" Here Master Simon made a pause, pulled up a tuft of flowers, and threw them one by one into the water,"—PAGE 165

a little upon the tender passion, and made sundry very excellent, though rather trite, observations upon disappointments in love. It was evident that he had something on his mind which he wished to impart, but felt awkward in approaching it. I was curious to see to what this strain would lead; but I was determined not to assist him. Indeed, I mischievously pretended to turn the conversation, and talked of his usual topics, dogs, horses, and hunting; but he was very brief in his replies, and invariably got back, by hook or by crook, into the sentimental vein.

At length we came to a clump of trees that overhung a whispering brook, with a rustic bench at their feet. The trees were grievously scored with letters and devices, which had grown out of all shape and size by the growth of the bark : and it appeared that this grove had served as a kind of register of the family loves from time immemorial. Here Master Simon made a pause, pulled up a tuft of flowers, threw them one by one into the water, and at length, turning somewhat abruptly upon me, asked me if ever I had been in love. I confess the question startled me a little, as I am not over fond of making confessions of my amorous follies; and, above all, should never dream of choosing my friend Master Simon for a confidant. He did not wait, however, for a reply; the inquiry was merely a prelude to a confession on his own part, and after several circumlocutions and whimsical preambles, he fairly disburthened himself of a very tolerable story of his having been crossed in love.

The reader will, very probably, suppose that it related to the gay widow who jilted him not long since at Doncaster races;—no such thing. It was about a sentimental passion that he once had for a most beautiful young lady, who wrote poetry and played on the harp. He used to serenade her; and indeed he described several tender and gallant scenes, in which he was evidently picturing himself in his mind's eye as some elegant hero of romance, though, unfortunately for the tale, I only saw him as he stood before me, a dapper little old bachelor, with a face like an apple that has dried with the bloom on it.

What were the particulars of this tender tale I have already forgotten; indeed I listened to it with a heart like a very pebble stone, having hard work to repress a smile while Master Simon was putting on the amorous swain, uttering every now and then a sigh, and endeavouring to look sentimental and melancholy.

All that I recollect is, that the lady, according to his account, was certainly a little touched; for she used to accept all the music that he copied for her harp, and all the patterns that he drew for her dresses; and he began to flatter himself, after a long course of delicate attentions, that he was gradually fanning up a gentle flame in her heart, when she suddenly accepted the hand of a rich, boisterous, fox-hunting baronet, without either music or sentiment, who carried her by storm, after a fortnight's courtship.

Master Simon could not help concluding by some observation upon "modest merit," and the power of gold over the sex. As a remembrance of his passion, he pointed out a heart carved on the bark of one of the trees; but which, in the process of time, had grown out into a large excrescence; and he showed me a lock of her hair, which he wore in a true lover's knot, in a large gold brooch.

I have seldom met with an old bachelor that had not, at some time or other, his nonsensical moment, when he would become tender and sentimental, talk about the concerns of the heart, and have some confession of a delicate nature to make. Almost every man has some little trait of romance in his life, which he looks back to with fondness, and about which he is apt to grow garrulous occasionally. He recollects himself as he was at the time, young and gamesome; and forgets that his hearers have no other idea of the hero of the tale, but such as he may appear at the time of telling it; peradventure, a withered, whimsical, spindle-shanked old gentleman. With married men, it is true, this is not so frequently the case; their amorous romance is apt to decline after marriage; why, I cannot for the life of me imagine; but with a bachelor, though it may slumber, it never dies. It is always liable to break out again in transient flashes, and never so much as on a spring morning in the country; or on a winter evening, when seated in his solitary chamber, stirring up the fire and talking of matrimony.

The moment that Master Simon had gone through his confession, and, to use the common phrase, "had made a clean breast of it," he became quite himself again. He had settled the point which had been worrying his mind, and doubtless considered himself established as a man of sentiment in my opinion. Before we had finished our morning's stroll, he was singing as blithe as a grasshopper, whistling to his dogs, and telling droll stories; and I recollect that he was particularly facetious that day at dinner on the subject of matrimony, and uttered several excellent jokes, not to be found in Joe Miller, that made the bride-elect blush and look down, but set all the old gentlemen at the table in a roar, and absolutely brought tears into the general's eyes.

GIPSIES.

What's that to absolute freedom, such as the very beggars have; to
feast and revel here to day, and yonder to-morrow; next day where
they please; and so on still, the whole country or kingdom over?
There's liberty ! the birds of the air can take no more.

JOVIAL CREW.

SINCE the meeting with the gipsies, which I have
related in a former paper, I have observed several
of them haunting the purlieus of the Hall, in spite
of a positive interdiction of the squire.   They are
part of a gang that has long kept about this
neighbourhood, to the great annoyance of the
farmers, whose poultry-yards often suffer from
their nocturnal invasions.   They are, however,

in some measure, patronised by the squire, who considers the race as belonging to the good old times ; which, to confess the private truth, seem to have abounded with good-for-nothing characters.

This roving crew is called "Starlight Tom's Gang," from the name of its chieftain, a notorious poacher. I have heard repeatedly of the misdeeds of this "minion of the moon;" for every midnight depredation that takes place in park, or fold, or farm-yard, is laid to his charge. Starlight Tom, in fact, answers to his name ; he seems to walk in darkness, and, like a fox, to be traced in the morning by the mischief he has done. He reminds me of that fearful personage in the nursery rhyme :

> " Who goes round the house at night?
>   None but bloody Tom !
> Who steals all the sheep at night?
>   None but one by one !"

In short, Starlight Tom is the scapegoat of the neighbourhood ; but so cunning and adroit, that there is no detecting him. Old Christy and the gamekeeper have watched many a night in hopes of entrapping him ; and Christy often patrols the park with his dogs, for the purpose, but all in

vain.   It is said that the squire winks hard at his
misdeeds, having an indulgent feeling towards the
vagabond, because of his being very expert at all
kinds of games, a great shot with the crossbow,
and the best morris dancer in the country.

The squire also suffers the gang to lurk unmolested about the skirts of his estate, on condition
that they do not come about the house.   The
approaching wedding, however, has made a kind
of Saturnalia at the Hall, and has caused a sus-
pension of all sober rule.   It has produced a
great sensation throughout the female part of the
household; not a housemaid but dreams of wedding favours, and has a husband running in her
head.   Such a time is a harvest for the gipsies:
there is a public footpath leading across one part
of the park, by which they have free ingress, and
they are continually hovering about the grounds,
telling the servant girls' fortunes, or getting
smuggled in to the young ladies.

I believe the Oxonian amuses himself very
much by furnishing them with hints in private,
and bewildering all the weak brains in the house
with their wonderful revelations.   The general
certainly was very much astonished by the com-

munications made to him the other evening by the gipsy girl : he kept a wary silence towards us on the subject, and affected to treat it lightly ; but I have noticed that he has since redoubled his attentions to Lady Lillycraft and her dogs.

I have seen also Phœbe Wilkins, the housekeeper's pretty and love-sick niece, holding a long conference with one of these old sibyls behind a large tree in the avenue, and often looking round to see that she was not observed. I make no doubt that she was endeavouring to get some favourable augury about the result of her love quarrel with young Ready-Money, as oracles have always been more consulted on love affairs than upon anything else. I fear, however, that in this instance the response was not so favourable as usual, for I perceived poor Phœbe returning pensively towards the house ; her head hanging down, her hat in her hand, and the riband trailing along the ground.

At another time, as I turned a corner of a terrace, at the bottom of the garden, just by a clump of trees, and a large stone urn, I came upon a bevy of the young girls of the family,

attended by this same Phœbe Wilkins.　I was at
a loss to comprehend the meaning of their blushing and giggling, and their apparent agitation,
until I saw the red cloak of a gipsy vanishing
among the shrubbery.　A few moments after, I
caught sight of Master Simon and the Oxonian
stealing along one of the walks of the garden,
chuckling and laughing at their successful waggery;
having evidently put the gipsy up to the thing,
and instructed her what to say.

　　After all, there is something strangely pleasing

in these tamperings with the future, even where we are convinced of the fallacy of the prediction. It is singular how willingly the mind will half deceive itself, and with what a degree of awe we will listen even to these babblers about futurity. For my part, I cannot feel angry with these poor vagabonds, that seek to deceive us into bright hopes and expectations. I have always been something of a castle-builder, and have found my liveliest pleasures to arise from the illusions which fancy has cast over commonplace realities. As I get on in life, I find it more difficult to deceive myself in this delightful manner; and I should be thankful to any prophet, however false, that would conjure the clouds which hang over futurity into palaces, and all its doubtful regions into fairyland.

The squire, who, as I have observed, has a private goodwill towards gipsies, has suffered considerable annoyance on their account. Not that they requite his indulgence with ingratitude, for they do not depredate very flagrantly on his estate; but because their pilferings and misdeeds occasion loud murmurs in the village. I can readily understand the old gentleman's humour on this point; I have a great toleration for all kinds of vagrant, sunshiny existence, and must confess I take a pleasure in observing the ways of gipsies. The English, who are accustomed to them from childhood, and often suffer from their petty depredations, consider them as mere nuisances; but I have been very much struck with their peculiarities. I like to behold their clear olive complexions, their romantic black eyes, their raven locks, their lithe, slender figures, and to hear them, in low, silver tones, dealing forth magnificent promises, of honours and estates, of world's worth, and ladies' love.

Their mode of life, too, has something in it very fanciful and picturesque. They are the free denizens of nature, and maintain a primitive independence, in spite of law and gospel; of county gaols and country magistrates. It is curious to see the obstinate adherence to the wild, unsettled habits of savage life transmitted from generation to generation, and preserved in the midst of one of the most cultivated, populous, and systematic countries in the world. They are totally distinct from the busy, thrifty people about them. They seem to be like the Indians of America, either above or below the ordinary cares and anxieties

of mankind.   Heedless of power, of honours, of
wealth ; and indifferent to the fluctuations of the
times, the rise or fall of grain, or stock, or empires,
they seem to laugh at the toiling, fretting world
around them, and to live according to the philosophy of the old song :

> " Who would ambition shun,
> And loves to lie i' the sun,
> Seeking the food he eats,
> And pleased with what he gets,
> Come hither, come hither, come hither ;
>   Here shall he see
>   No enemy,
> But winter and rough weather."

In this way they wander from county to
county, keeping about the purlieus of villages, or
in plenteous neighbourhoods, where there are fat
farms and rich country seats.   Their encampments
are generally made in some beautiful spot ; either
a green shady nook of a road ; or on the border
of a common, under a sheltering hedge ; or on the
skirts of a fine spreading wood.   They are always
to be found lurking about fairs and races, and
rustic gatherings, wherever there is pleasure, and
throng, and idleness.   They are the oracles of
milkmaids and simple serving girls ; and sometimes have even the honour of perusing the white

hands of gentlemen's daughters, when rambling about their father's grounds. They are the bane of good housewives and thrifty farmers, and odious in the eyes of country justices; but, like all other vagabond beings, they have something to commend them to the fancy. They are among the last traces, in these mattter-of-fact days, of the motley population of former times; and are whimsically associated in my mind with fairies and witches, Robin Goodfellow, Robin Hood, and the other fantastical personages of poetry.

VILLAGE WORTHIES.

Nay, I tell you, I am so well beloved in our town, that not the worst
dog in the street would hurt my little finger.

COLLIER OF CROYDON.

As the neighbouring village is one of those out-of-
the-way, but gossiping little places, where a small
matter makes a great stir, it is not to be supposed
that the approach of a festival like that of May-
Day can be regarded with indifference, especially
since it is made a matter of such moment by the
great folks at the Hall.   Master Simon, who is
the faithful factotum of the worthy squire, and
jumps with his humour in everything, is frequent
just now in his visits to the village, to give directions for the impending fête; and as I have taken

the liberty occasionally of accompanying him, I have been enabled to get some insight into the characters and internal politics of this very sagacious little community.

Master Simon is in fact the Cæsar of the village. It is true the squire is the protecting power, but his factotum is the active and busy agent. He intermeddles in all its concerns, is acquainted with all the inhabitants and their domestic history, gives counsel to the old folks in their business matters, and the young folks in their love affairs, and enjoys the proud satisfaction of being a great man in a little world.

He is the dispenser, too, of the squire's charity, which is bounteous; and, to do Master Simon justice, he performs this part of his functions with great alacrity. Indeed I have been entertained with the mixture of bustle, importance, and kindheartedness which he displays. He is of too vivacious a temperament to comfort the afflicted by sitting down moping and whining and blowing noses in concert; but goes whisking about like a sparrow, chirping consolation into every hole and corner of the village. I have seen an old woman, in a red cloak, hold him for half an hour together with

some long phthisical tale of distress, which Master Simon listened to with many a bob of the head, smack of his dog-whip, and other symptoms of impatience, though he afterwards made a most faithful and circumstantial report of the case to the squire. I have watched him, too, during one of his pop visits into the cottage of a superannuated villager, who is a pen-
sioner of the squire, when he fidgeted about the room with-out sitting down, made many excellent off-hand reflections with the old invalid, who was propped up in his chair, about the shortness of life, the certainty of death, and the necessity of pre-paring for "that awful change;" quoted seve-ral texts of Scripture

very incorrectly, but much to the edification of the cottager's wife; and on coming out pinched the daughter's rosy cheek, and wondered what was in the young men, that such a pretty face did not get a husband.

He has also his cabinet councillors in the village, with whom he is very busy just now, preparing for the May-Day ceremonies. Among these is the village tailor, a pale-faced fellow, that plays the clarionet in the church choir; and, being a great musical genius, has frequent meetings of the band at his house, where they "make night hideous" by their concerts. He is, in consequence, high in favour with Master Simon; and, through his influence, has the making, or rather marring, of all the liveries of the Hall; which generally look as though they had been cut out by one of those scientific tailors of the Flying Island of Laputa, who took measure of their customers with a quadrant. The tailor, in fact, might rise to be one of the monied men of the village, was he not rather too prone to gossip, and keep holidays, and give concerts, and blow all his substance, real and personal, through his clarionet, which literally keeps him poor both in body and estate. He has for the present thrown by all his regular work, and suffered the breeches of the village to go unmade and unmended, while he is occupied in making garlands of parti-coloured rags, in imitation of flowers, for the decoration of the May-pole.

Another of Master Simon's councillors is the apothecary, a short, and rather fat man, with a

pair of prominent eyes, that diverge like those of a lobster. He is the village wise man; very sententious; and full of profound remarks on shallow subjects. Master Simon often quotes his sayings, and mentions him as rather an extra-ordinary man; and even consults him occasionally in desperate cases of the dogs and horses. Indeed he seems to have been overwhelmed by the apothecary's philosophy, which is exactly one observation deep, consisting of indisputable maxims, such as may be gathered from the mottoes of tobacco boxes. I had a specimen of his philosophy in my very first conversation with him; in the course of which he observed, with great solemnity and emphasis, that "man is a compound of wisdom and folly;" upon which Master Simon, who had hold of my arm, pressed very hard upon it, and whispered in my ear, "That's a devilish shrewd remark!"

THE SCHOOLMASTER

There will no mosse stick to the stone of Sisiphus, no grasse hang on the heels of Mercury, no butter cleave on the bread of a traveller. For as the eagle at every flight loseth a feather, which maketh her bauld in her age, so the traveller in every country loseth some fleece, which maketh him a beggar in his youth, by buying that for a pound which he cannot sell again for a penny—repentance.

LILLY'S EUPHUES.

AMONG the worthies of the village, that enjoy the peculiar confidence of Master Simon, is one who has struck my fancy so much that I have thought him worthy of a separate notice. It is Slingsby, the schoolmaster, a thin, elderly man, rather threadbare and slovenly, somewhat indolent in manner, and with an easy, good-humoured look, not often met with in his craft. I have been interested in his favour by a few anecdotes which I have picked up concerning him.

He is a native of the village, and was a contemporary and playmate of Ready-Money Jack in the days of their boyhood. Indeed, they carried on a kind of league of mutual good offices. Slingsby was rather puny, and withal somewhat of a coward, but very apt at his learning ; Jack, on the contrary, was a bully-boy out of doors, but a sad laggard at his books. Slingsby helped Jack, therefore, to all his lessons : Jack fought all Slingsby's battles ; and they were inseparable friends. This mutual kindness continued even after they left school, notwithstanding the dissimilarity of their characters. Jack took to ploughing and reaping, and prepared himself to till his paternal acres ; while the other loitered negligently on in the path of learning, until he penetrated even into the confines of Latin and mathematics.

In an unlucky hour, however, he took to reading voyages and travels, and was smitten with a desire to see the world. This desire increased upon him as he grew up ; so, early one bright, sunny morning, he put all his effects in a knapsack, slung it on his back, took staff in hand, and called in his way to take leave of his early schoolmate. Jack was just going out with the plough : the friends shook hands over the farm-house gate ;

Jack drove his team afield, and Slingsby whistled "Over the hills, and far away," and sallied forth gaily to "seek his fortune."

Years and years passed by, and young Tom Slingsby was forgotten: when, one mellow Sunday afternoon in autumn, a thin man, somewhat advanced in life, with a coat out at elbows, a pair of old nankeen gaiters, and a few things tied in a handkerchief, and slung on the end of a stick, was seen loitering through the village. He appeared to regard several houses attentively, to peer into the windows that were open, to eye the villagers wistfully as they returned from church, and then to pass some time in the churchyard, reading the tombstones.

At length he found his way to the farm-house of Ready-Money Jack, but paused ere he attempted the wicket; contemplating the picture of substantial independence before him. In the porch of the house sat Ready-Money Jack, in his Sunday dress, with his hat upon his head, his pipe in his mouth, and his tankard before him, the monarch of all he surveyed. Beside him lay his fat house-dog. The varied sounds of poultry were heard from the well-stocked farm-yard; the bees hummed from their hives in the garden; the cattle lowed in the rich meadow: while the crammed barns and ample stacks bore proof of an abundant harvest.

The stranger opened the gate and advanced dubiously towards the house. The mastiff growled at the sight of the suspicious-looking intruder, but was immediately silenced by his master, who, taking his pipe from his mouth, awaited with inquiring aspect the address of this equivocal personage. The stranger eyed old Jack for a moment, so portly in his dimensions, and decked out in gorgeous apparel; then cast a glance upon his own threadbare and starveling condition, and the scanty bundle which he held in his hand; then giving his shrunk waistcoat a twitch to make it meet his receding waistband; and casting another look, half sad, half humorous at the sturdy yeoman, "I suppose," said he, "Mr. Tibbets, you have forgot old times and old playmates?"

The latter gazed at him with scrutinizing look, but acknowledged that he had no recollection of him.

"Like enough, like enough," said the stranger;

"Why, no sure! it can't be Tom Slingsby?" —PAGE 189.

" everybody seems to have forgotten poor Slings-by ?"

"Why, no sure! it can't be Tom Slingsby ?"

"Yes, but it is, though!" replied the stranger, shaking his head.

Ready-Money Jack was on his feet in a twink-ling; thrust out his hand, gave his ancient crony the gripe of a giant, and slapping the other hand on a bench, "Sit down there," cried he, "Tom Slingsby!"

A long conversation ensued about old times, while Slingsby was regaled with the best cheer that the farm-house afforded; for he was hungry as well as wayworn, and had the keen appetite of a poor pedestrian. The early playmates then talked over their subsequent lives and adventures. Jack had but little to relate, and was never good at a long story. A prosperous life, passed at home, has little incident for narrative; it is only poor devils, that are tossed about the world, that are the true heroes of story. Jack had stuck by the paternal farm, followed the same plough that his forefathers had driven, and had waxed richer and richer as he grew older. As to Tom Slingsby, he was an exemplification of the old proverb, " A rolling stone gathers no moss." He had sought his fortune about the world, without ever finding it, being a thing oftener found at home than abroad. He had been in all kinds of situations, and had learned a dozen different modes of making a living; but had found his way back to his native village rather poorer than when he left it, his knapsack having dwindled down to a scanty bundle.

As luck would have it, the squire was passing by the farm-house that very evening, and called there, as is often his custom. He found the two schoolmates still gossiping in the porch, and, according to the good old Scottish song, "taking a cup of kindness yet, for auld lang syne." The squire was struck by the contrast in appearance and fortunes of these early playmates. Ready-Money Jack, seated in lordly state, surrounded by the good things of this life, with golden guineas hanging to his very watch chain, and the poor pilgrim Slingsby, thin as a weasel, with all his worldly effects, his bundle, hat, and walking-staff, lying on the ground beside him.

The good squire's heart warmed towards the luckless cosmopolite, for he is a little prone to like such half-vagrant characters. He cast about in his mind how he should contrive once more to anchor Slingsby in his native village. Honest Jack had already offered him a present shelter under his roof, in spite of the hints, and winks, and half remonstrances of the shrewd Dame Tibbets; but how to provide for his permanent maintenance was the question. Luckily the squire bethought himself that the village school was without a teacher. A little further conversation convinced him that Slingsby was as fit for that as for anything else, and in a day or two he was seen swaying the rod of empire in the very school-house where he had often been horsed in the days of his boyhood.

Here he has remained for several years, and being honoured by the countenance of the squire, and the fast friendship of Mr. Tibbets, he has grown into much importance and consideration in the village. I am told, however, that he still shows, now and then, a degree of restlessness, and a disposition to rove abroad again, and see a little more of the world; an inclination which seems particularly to haunt him about spring-time. There is nothing so difficult to conquer as the vagrant humour, when once it has been fully indulged.

Since I have heard these anecdotes of poor Slingsby, I have more than once mused upon the picture presented by him and his schoolmate Ready-Money Jack, on their coming together again after so long a separation. It is difficult to determine between lots in life, where each is attended with its peculiar discontents. He who never leaves his home repines at his monotonous existence, and envies the traveller, whose life is a constant tissue of wonder and adventure; while he, who is tossed about the world, looks back with many a sigh to the safe and quiet shore which he has abandoned. I cannot help thinking, however, that the man that stays at home, and cultivates the comforts and pleasures daily springing up around him, stands the best chance for happiness. There is nothing so fascinating to a young mind as the idea of travelling; and there is very witchcraft in the old phrase found in every nursery tale, of "going to seek one's fortune." A continual change of place, and change of object, promises a continual succession of adventure and gratification of curiosity. But there is a limit to

all our enjoyments, and every desire bears its
death in its very gratification. Curiosity lan-
guishes under repeated stimulants, novelties cease
to excite surprise, until at length we cannot wonder
even at a miracle. He who has sallied forth into
the world, like poor Slingsby, full of sunny anti-
cipations, finds too soon how different the distant
scene becomes when visited. The smooth place
roughens as he approaches; the wild place becomes tame and barren; the fairy tints that
beguiled him on still fly to the distant hill, or
gather upon the land he has left behind, and every
part of the landscape seems greener than the spot
he stands on.

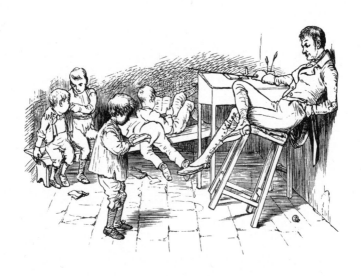

THE SCHOOL.

But to come down from great men and higher matters to my little children and poor school-house again; I will, God willing, go forward
orderly, as I proposed, to instruct children and young men both for
learning and manners.   ROGER ASCHAM.

HAVING given the reader a slight sketch of the
village schoolmaster, he may be curious to learn
something concerning his school. As the squire
takes much interest in the education of the neighbouring children, he put into the hands of the
teacher, on first installing him in office, a copy of
Roger Ascham's Schoolmaster, and advised him,
moreover, to con over that portion of old Peachum
which treats of the duty of masters, and which

condemns the favourite method of making boys wise by flagellation.

He exhorted Slingsby not to break down or depress the free spirit of the boys, by harshness and slavish fear, but to lead them freely and joyously on in the path of knowledge, making it pleasant and desirable in their eyes. He wished to see the youth trained up in the manners and habitudes of the peasantry of the good old times, and thus to lay the foundation for the accomplishment of his favourite object, the revival of old English customs and character. He recommended that all the ancient holidays should be observed, and that the sports of the boys, in their hours of play, should be regulated according to the standard authorities laid down by Strutt; a copy of whose invaluable work, decorated with plates, was deposited in the school-house. Above all, he exhorted the pedagogue to abstain from the use of birch, an instrument of instruction which the good squire regards with abhorrence, as fit only for the coercion of brute natures, that cannot be reasoned with.

Mr. Slingsby has followed the squire's instructions to the best of his disposition and abilities. He never flogs the boys, because he is too easy, good-humoured a creature to inflict pain on a worm. He is bountiful in holidays, because he loves holidays himself, and has a sympathy with the urchins' impatience of confinement, from having divers times experienced its irksomeness during the time that he was seeing the world. As to sports and pastimes, the boys are faithfully exercised in all that are on record,—quoits, races, prison-bars, tipcat, trap-ball, bandy-ball, wrestling, leaping, and what not. The only misfortune is, that having banished the birch, honest Slingsby has not studied Roger Ascham sufficiently to find out a substitute, or rather he has not the management in his nature to apply one ; his school, therefore, though one of the happiest, is one of the most unruly in the country ; and never was a pedagogue more liked, or less heeded, by his disciples than Slingsby.

He has lately taken a coadjutor worthy of himself, being another stray sheep that has returned to the village fold. This is no other than the son of the musical tailor, who had bestowed some cost upon his education, hoping to see him one day arrive at the dignity of an exciseman, or at least of a parish clerk. The lad grew up, however, as idle and musical as his father; and, being captivated by the drum and fife of a recruiting party, he followed them off to the army. He returned not long since, out of money, and out at elbows, the prodigal son of the village.

He remained for some time lounging about the place in half-tattered soldier's dress, with a foraging cap on one side of his head, jerking stones across the brook, or loitering about the tavern door, a burthen to his father, and regarded with great coldness by all warm householders.

Something, however, drew honest Slingsby towards the youth. It might be the kindness he bore to his father, who is one of the schoolmaster's greatest cronies ; it might be that secret sympathy, which draws men of vagrant propensities towards each other ; for there is something truly magnetic in the vagabond feeling ; or it might be, that he remembered the time when he himself had come back, like this youngster, a wreck to his native place. At any rate, whatever the motive, Slingsby drew towards the youth. They had many conversations in the village tap-room about foreign parts, and the various scenes and places they had witnessed during their wayfaring about the world. The more Slingsby talked with him, the more he found him to his taste, and finding him almost as learned as himself, he forthwith engaged him as an assistant or usher in the school.

Under such admirable tuition, the school, as may be supposed, flourishes apace ; and if the scholars do not become versed in all the holiday accomplishments of the good old times, to the squire's heart's content, it will not be the fault of their teachers. The prodigal son has become almost as popular among the boys as the peda-gogue himself. His instructions are not limited to school hours; and having inherited the musical taste and talents of his father, he has bitten the whole school with the mania. He is a great hand at beating a drum, which is often heard rumbling from the rear of the school-house. He is teaching half the boys of the village, also, to play the fife, and the pandean pipes; and they weary the whole neighbourhood with their vague piping, as they sit perched on stiles, or loitering about the barn-doors in the evenings. Among the other exercises of the school, also, he has introduced the ancient art of archery, one of the squire's favourite themes, with such success, that the whipsters roam in truant bands about the neigh-bourhood, practising with their bows and arrows upon the birds of the air, and the beasts of the field; and not unfrequently making a foray into the squire's domains, to the great indignation of the gamekeepers. In a word, so completely are the ancient English customs and habits cultivated at this school, that I should not be surprised

if the squire should live to see one of his
poetic visions realised, and a brood reared up,
worthy successors to Robin Hood and his merry
gang of outlaws.

A VILLAGE POLITICIAN.

I am a rogue if I do not think I was designed for the helm of state ; I am
  so full of nimble stratagems, that I should have ordered affairs, and
  carried it against the stream of a faction, with as much ease as a
  skipper would laver against the wind. —THE GOBLINS.

IN one of my visits to the village with Master
Simon, he proposed that we should stop at the
inn, which he wished to show me, as a specimen
of a real country inn, the head-quarters of village
gossip. I had remarked it before, in my per-
ambulations about the place. It has a deep, old-
fashioned porch, leading into a large hall, which
serves for tap-room and travellers' room ; having a
wide fireplace, with high-backed settles on each
side, where the wise men of the village gossip
over their ale, and hold their sessions during the
long winter evenings. The landlord is an easy,
indolent fellow, shaped a little like one of his own

beer barrels, and is apt to stand gossiping at his door, with his wig on one side, and his hands in his pockets, whilst his wife and daughter attend to customers. His wife, however, is fully competent to manage the establishment; and, indeed, from long habitude, rules over all the frequenters of the tap-room as completely as if they were her dependants instead of her patrons. Not a veteran ale-bibber but pays homage to her, having, no doubt, been often in her arrears. I have already hinted that she is on very good terms with Ready-Money Jack. He was a sweetheart of hers in early life, and has always countenanced the tavern on her account. Indeed, he is quite "the cock of the walk" at the tap-room.

As we approached the inn, we heard some one talking with great volubility, and distinguished the ominous words "taxes," "poor's rates," and "agricultural distress." It proved to be a thin, loquacious fellow, who had penned the landlord up in one corner of the porch, with his hands in his pockets as usual, listening with an air of the most vacant acquiescence.

The sight seemed to have a curious effect on Master Simon, as he squeezed my arm, and, altering his course, sheered wide of the porch as though he had not had any idea of entering. This evident evasion induced me to notice the orator more particularly. He was meagre, but active in his make, with a long, pale, bilious face; a black, ill-shaven beard, a feverish eye, and a hat sharpened up at the sides into a most pragmatical shape. He had a newspaper in his hand, and seemed to be commenting on its contents, to the thorough conviction of mine host.

At sight of Master Simon the landlord was evidently a little flurried, and began to rub his hands, edge away from his corner, and make several profound publican bows; while the orator took no other notice of my companion than to talk rather louder than before, and with, as I thought, something of an air of defiance. Master Simon, however, as I have before said, sheered off from the porch, and passed on, pressing my arm within his, and whispering as we got by, in a tone of awe and horror, "That's a radical! he reads Cobbett!"

I endeavoured to get a more particular account of him from my companion, but he seemed un-willing even to talk about him, answering only in general terms, that he was "a cursed busy fellow, that had a confounded trick of talking, and was apt to bother one about the national debt, and such nonsense;" from which I suspected that Master Simon had been rendered wary of him by some accidental encounter on the field of argument: for these radicals are continually roving about in quest of wordy warfare, and never so happy as when they can tilt a gentleman logician out of his saddle.

On subsequent inquiry my suspicions have been confirmed. I find the radical has but recently found his way into the village, where he threatens to commit fearful devastations with his doctrines. He has already made two or three complete converts, or new lights; has shaken the faith of several others; and has grievously puzzled the brains of many of the oldest villagers, who had never thought about politics, or scarce anything else, during their whole lives.

He is lean and meagre from the constant restlessness of mind and body; worrying about with newspapers and pamphlets in his pockets, which he is ready to pull out on all occasions. He has shocked several of the staunchest villagers by talking lightly of the squire and his family;

and hinting that it would be better the park should be cut up into small farms and kitchen gardens, or feed good mutton instead of worthless deer.

He is a great thorn in the side of the squire, who is sadly afraid that he will introduce politics into the village, and turn it into an unhappy, thinking community. He is a still greater grievance to Master Simon, who has hitherto been able to sway the political opinions of the place, without much cost of learning or logic ; but has been very much puzzled of late to weed out the doubts and heresies already sown by this champion of reform. Indeed, the latter has taken complete command at the tap-room of the tavern, not so much because he has convinced, as because he has out-talked all the established oracles. The apothecary, with all his philosophy, was as nought before him. He has convinced and converted the landlord at least a dozen times; who, however, is liable to be convinced and converted the other way by the next person with whom he talks. It is true the radical

has a violent antagonist in the landlady, who is vehemently loyal, and thoroughly devoted to the king, Master Simon, and the squire. She now and then comes out upon the reformer with all the fierceness of a cat-o'-mountain, and does not spare her own soft-headed husband, for listening to what she terms such "low-lived politics." What makes the good woman the more violent, is the perfect coolness with which the radical listens to her attacks, drawing his face up into a provoking supercilious smile; and when she has talked herself out of breath, quietly asking her for a taste of her home-brewed.

The only person who is in any way a match for this redoubtable politician is Ready-Money Jack Tibbets, who maintains his stand in the tap-room, in defiance of the radical and all his works. Jack is one of the most loyal men in the country, without being able to reason about the matter. He has that admirable quality for a tough arguer, also, that he never knows when he is beat. He has half-a dozen old maxims, which he advances on all occasions, and though his antagonist may overturn them never so often, yet he always brings them anew into the field. He is like the robber in Ariosto, who, though his head might be cut off half a hundred times, yet whipped it on his shoulders again in a twinkling, and returned as sound a man as ever to the charge.

Whatever does not square with Jack's simple and obvious creed, he sets down for " French politics ; " for, notwithstanding the peace, he cannot be persuaded that the French are not still laying plots to ruin the nation, and to get hold of the Bank of England. The radical attempted to overwhelm him one day by a long passage from a newspaper ; but Jack neither reads nor believes on newspapers. In reply he gave him one of the stanzas which he has by heart from his favourite, and indeed only author, old Tusser, and which he calls his Golden Rules :

> Leave Princes' affairs undescanted on,
> And tend to such doings as stand thee upon ;
> Fear God, and offend not the King nor his laws,
> And keep thyself out of the magistrate's claws.

When Tibbets had pronounced this with great emphasis, he pulled out a well-filled leathern purse, took out a handful of gold and silver, paid his score at the bar with great punctuality, returned his money, piece by piece, into his purse, his purse into his pocket, which he buttoned up, and then giving his cudgel a stout thump upon the floor, and bidding the radical "Good morning, sir!" with the tone of a man who conceives he has completely done for his antagonist, he walked with lion-like gravity out of the house. Two or three of Jack's admirers who were present, and had been afraid to take the field themselves, looked upon this as a perfect triumph, and winked at each other when the radical's back was turned. "Ay, ay!" said mine host, as soon as the radical was out of hearing, "let old Jack alone; I'll warrant he'll give him his own!"

THE ROOKERY

But cawing rooks, and kites that swim sublime
In still repeated circles, screaming loud,
The jay, the pie, and e'en the boding owl,
That hails the rising moon, have charms for me.
                                        COWPER.

IN a grove of tall oaks and beeches, that crowns a
terrace walk, just on the skirts of the garden, is an
ancient rookery, which is one of the most important
provinces in the squire's rural domains. The old
gentleman sets great store by his rooks, and will
not suffer one of them to be killed, in consequence
of which they have increased amazingly; the tree
tops are loaded with their nests; they have en-
croached upon the great avenue, and have even
established, in times long past, a colony among
the elms and pines of the churchyard, which, like
other distant colonies, has already thrown off
allegiance to the mother-country.

The rooks are looked upon by the squire as a very ancient and honourable line of gentry, highly aristocratical in their notions, fond of place, and attached to church and state; as their building so loftily, keeping about churches and cathedrals, and in the venerable groves of old castles and manor-houses, sufficiently manifests. The good opinion thus expressed by the squire put me upon observing more narrowly these very respectable birds; for I confess, to my shame, I had been apt to confound them with their cousins-german the crows, to whom, at the first glance, they bear so great a family resemblance. Nothing, it seems, could be more unjust or injurious than such a mistake. The rooks and crows are, among the feathered tribes, what the Spaniards and Portuguese are among nations, the least loving, in consequence of their neighbourhood and similarity The rooks are old-established housekeepers, high-minded gentlefolk that have had their hereditary abodes time out of mind; but as to the poor crows, they are a kind of vagabond, predatory, gipsy race, roving about the country, without any settled home; "their hands are against everybody, and everybody's against them," and they are gibbeted in every corn-field. Master Simon assures me that a female rook that should so far forget herself as to consort with a crow, would inevitably be disinherited, and indeed would be totally discarded by all her genteel acquaintance.

The squire is very watchful over the interests and concerns of his sable neighbours. As to Master Simon, he even pretends to know many of them by sight, and to have given names to them; he points out several which he says are old heads of families, and compares them to worthy old citizens, beforehand in the world, that wear cocked hats and silver buckles in their shoes. Notwithstanding the protecting benevolence of the squire, and their being residents in his empire, they seem to acknowledge no allegiance, and to hold no intercourse or intimacy. Their airy tenements are built almost out of the reach of gun-shot; and, notwithstanding their vicinity to the Hall, they maintain a most reserved and distrustful shyness of mankind.

There is one season of the year, however, which brings all birds in a manner to a level, and tames the pride of the loftiest highflyer; which is the season of building their nests. This takes place early in the spring, when the forest trees first begin to show their buds; the long withy ends of the branches to turn green; when the wild strawberry, and other herbage of the sheltered woodlands, put forth their tender and tinted leaves, and the daisy and the primrose peep from under the hedges. At this time there is a general bustle among the feathered tribes; an incessant fluttering about, and a cheerful chirping, indicative, like the germination of the vegetable world, of the reviving life and fecundity of the year.

It is then that the rooks forget their usual stateliness, and their shy and lofty habits. Instead of keeping up in the high regions of the air, swinging on the breezy tree tops, and looking down with sovereign contempt upon the humble crawlers upon earth, they are fain to throw off for a time the dignity of a gentleman, and to come down to the ground, and put on the painstaking and industrious character of a labourer. They now lose their natural shyness, become fearless and familiar, and may be seen flying about in all directions, with an air of great assiduity, in search of building materials. Every now and then your path will be crossed by one of these busy old

gentlemen, worrying about with awkward gait, as
if troubled with the gout or with corns on his toes,
casting about many a prying look, turning down
first one eye, then the other, in earnest consideration upon every straw he meets with, until espying
some mighty twig, large enough to make a rafter
for his air-castle, he will seize upon it with avidity,
and hurry away with it to the tree top; fearing,
apparently, lest you should dispute with him the
invaluable prize.

Like other castle-builders, these airy architects
seem rather fanciful in the materials with which

they build, and to like those most which come from a distance. Thus, though there are abundance of dry twigs on the surrounding trees, yet they never think of making use of them, but go foraging in distant lands, and come sailing home, one by one, from the ends of the earth, each bearing in his bill some precious piece of timber.

Nor must I avoid mentioning what, I grieve to say, rather derogates from the grave and honourable character of these ancient gentlefolk, that, during the architectural season, they are subject to great dissensions among themselves; that they make no scruple to defraud and plunder each other; and that sometimes the rookery is a scene of hideous brawl and commotion, in consequence of some delinquency of the kind. One of the partners generally remains on the nest to guard it from depredation; and I have seen severe contests when some sly neighbour has endeavoured to filch away a tempting rafter that has captivated his eye. As I am not willing to admit any suspicion hastily that should throw a stigma on the general character of so worshipful a people, I am inclined to think that these larcenies are very much discountenanced by the higher classes, and even rigorously punished by those in authority; for I have now and then seen a whole gang of rooks fall upon the nest of some individual, pull it all to pieces, carry off the spoils, and even buffet the luckless proprietor. I have concluded this to be some signal punishment inflicted upon him by the officers of the police, for some pilfering misdemeanour; or, perhaps, that it was a crew of bailiffs carrying an execution into his house.

I have been amused with another of their movements during the building season. The steward has suffered a considerable number of sheep to graze on a lawn near the house, somewhat to the annoyance of the squire, who thinks this an innovation on the dignity of a park, which ought to be devoted to deer only. Be this as it may, there is a green knoll, not far from the drawing-room window, were the ewes and lambs are accustomed to assemble towards evening for the benefit of the setting sun. No sooner were they gathered here, at the time when these politic birds were building, than a stately old rook, who, Master Simon assured me, was the chief magistrate of this community, would settle down upon the head of one of the ewes, who, seeming conscious of this condescension, would desist from grazing, and stand fixed in motionless reverence of her august brethren ; the rest of the rookery would then come wheeling down, in imitation of their leader, until every ewe had two or three of them cawing, and fluttering, and battling upon her back. Whether they requited the submission of the sheep by levying a contribution upon their fleece for the benefit of the rookery, I am not certain, though I presume they followed the usual custom of protecting powers.

The latter part of May is a time of great tribulation among the rookeries, when the young are just able to leave the nests, and balance themselves on the neighbouring branches. Now comes on the season of "rook shooting :" a terrible slaughter of the innocents. The squire, of course, prohibits all invasion of the kind on his territories; but I am told that a lamentable havoc takes place in the colony about the old church. Upon this devoted commonwealth the village charges "with all its chivalry." Every idle wight that is lucky enough to possess an old gun or a blunderbuss, together with all the archery of Slingsby's school, take the field on the occasion. In vain does the little parson interfere, or remonstrate in angry tones, from his study window that looks into the churchyard ; there is a continual popping from morning to night. Being no great marksmen, their shots are not often effective ; but every now and then a great shout from the besieging army of bumpkins makes known the downfall of some unlucky, squab rook, which comes to the ground with the emphasis of a squashed apple-dumpling.

Nor is the rookery entirely free from other troubles and disasters. In so aristocratical and lofty-minded a community, which boasts so much ancient blood and hereditary pride, it is natural to suppose that questions of etiquette will sometimes arise, and affairs of honour ensue.   In fact, this is very often the case : bitter quarrels break out between individuals, which produce sad scufflings on the tree tops, and I have more than once seen a regular duel take place between two doughty heroes of the rookery.   Their field of battle is generally the air : and their contest is managed in the most scientific and elegant manner ; wheeling round and round each other, and towering higher and higher to get the 'vantage ground, until they sometimes disappear in the clouds before the combat is determined.

They have also fierce combats now and then with an invading hawk, and will drive him off from their territories by a *posse comitatus*.   They are also extremely tenacious of their domains, and will suffer no other bird to inhabit the grove or its vicinity.   There was a very ancient and respectable old bachelor owl that had long had his lodgings in a corner of the grove, but has been fairly ejected by the rooks, and has retired, disgusted with the world, to a neighbouring wood,

where he leads the life of a hermit, and makes nightly complaints of his ill-treatment.

The hootings of this unhappy gentleman may generally be heard in the still evenings, when the rooks are all at rest; and I have often listened to them of a moonlight night, with a kind of mysterious gratification. This gray-bearded mis-anthrope of course is highly respected by the squire, but the servants have superstitious notions about him; and it would be difficult to get the dairymaid to venture after dark near to the wood which he inhabits.

Besides the private quarrels of the rooks, there are other misfortunes to which they are liable, and which often bring distress into the most respectable families of the rookery. Having the true baronial spirit of the good old feudal times, they are apt now and then to issue forth from their castles on a foray, and to lay the plebeian fields of the neighbouring country under contribution; in the course of which chivalrous expeditions they now and then get a shot from the rusty artillery of some refractory farmer. Occasionally, too, while they are quietly taking the air beyond the park boundaries, they have the incaution to come within the reach of the truant bowmen of Slingsby's school, and receive a flight shot from some unlucky urchin's arrow. In such case the wounded adventurer will sometimes have just strength enough to bring himself home, and giving up the ghost at the rookery, will hang dangling "all abroad" on a bough like a thief on a gibbet; an awful warning to his friends, and

an object of great commiseration to the squire.
But, maugre all these untoward incidents, the rooks
have, upon the whole, a happy holiday life of it.
When their young are reared, and fairly launched
upon their native element, the air, the cares of the
old folks seem over, and they resume all their
aristocratical dignity and idleness. I have envied
them the enjoyment which they appear to have in
their ethereal heights, sporting with clamorous
exultation about their lofty bowers ; sometimes
hovering over them, sometimes partially alighting
upon the topmost branches, and there balancing
with outstretched wings, and swinging in the
breeze. Sometimes they seem to take a fashionable drive to the church, and amuse themselves
by circling in airy rings about its spire : at other
times a mere garrison is left at home to mount
guard in their stronghold at the grove, while the
rest roam abroad to enjoy the fine weather.
About sunset the garrison gives notice of their
return ; their faint cawing will be heard from a
great distance, and they will be seen far off like a
sable cloud, and then nearer and nearer, until they
all come soaring home. Then they perform
several grand circuits in the air, over the Hall

and garden, wheeling closer and closer, until they gradually settle down upon the grove, when a prodigious cawing takes place, as though they were relating their day's adventures.

I like at such times to walk about these dusky groves, and hear the various sounds of these airy people roosted so high above me. As the gloom increases, their conversation subsides, and they seem to be gradually dropping asleep; but every now and then there is a querulous note, as if some one was quarrelling for a pillow, or a little more of the blanket. It is late in the evening before they completely sink to repose, and then their old anchorite neighbour, the owl, begins his lonely hootings from his bachelor's hall in the wood.

MAY-DAY.

It is the choice time of the year,
For the violets now appear;
Now the rose receives its birth,
And pretty primrose decks the earth.
Then to the May-pole come away,
For it is now a holiday.

ACTÆON AND DIANA.

As I was lying in bed this morning, enjoying one of those half-dreams, half-reveries, which are so pleasant in the country, when the birds are singing about the window, and the sunbeams peeping through the curtains, I was roused by the sound of music. On going down-stairs, I found a number of villagers dressed in their holiday clothes, bearing a pole ornamented with garlands and ribands, and accompanied by the village band of

music, under the direction of the tailor, the pale
fellow who plays on the clarionet. They had all
sprigs of hawthorn, or, as it is called, "the May,"
in their hats, and had brought green branches and
flowers to decorate the Hall door and windows.
They had come to give notice that the May-pole
was reared on the green, and to invite the household to witness the sports. The Hall, according
to custom, became a scene of hurry and delightful
confusion. The servants were all agog with May
and music; and there was no keeping either the
tongues or the feet of the maids quiet, who were
anticipating the sports of the green, and the evening dance.

I repaired to the village at an early hour to
enjoy the merry-making. The morning was pure
and sunny, such as a May morning is always
described. The fields were white with daisies, the
hawthorn was covered with its fragrant blossoms,
the bee hummed about every bank, and the swallow
played high in the air about the village steeple. It
was one of those genial days when we seem to
draw in pleasure with the very air we breathe, and
to feel happy we know not why. Whoever has
felt the worth of worthy man, or has doted on

Q

lovely woman, will, on such a day, call them tenderly to mind, and feel his heart all alive with long-buried recollections. " For thenne," says the excellent romance of King Arthur, "lovers call ageyne to their mynde old gentilnes and old servyse, and many kind dedes that were forgotten by neglygence."

Before reaching the village, I saw the May-pole towering above the cottages, with its gay garlands and streamers, and heard the sound of music. I found that there had been booths set up near it, for the reception of company ; and a bower of green branches and flowers for the Queen of May, a fresh, rosy-cheeked girl of the village.

A band of morris-dancers were capering on the green in their fantastic dresses, jingling with hawks' bells, with a boy dressed up as Maid Marian, and the attendant fool rattling his box to collect contributions from the bystanders. The gipsy women, too, were already plying their mystery in by-corners of the village, reading the hands of the simple country girls, and no doubt promising them all good husbands and tribes of children.

The squire made his appearance in the course of the morning, attended by the parson, and was received with loud acclamations. He mingled among the country people throughout the day, giving and receiving pleasure wherever he went. The amusements of the day were under the management of Slingsby, the schoolmaster, who is not merely lord of misrule in his school, but master of the revels to the village. He was bustling about with the perplexed and anxious air of a man who has the oppressive burthen of promoting other people's merriment upon his mind. He had involved himself in a dozen scrapes in consequence of a politic intrigue, which, by the by, Master Simon and the Oxonian were at the bottom of, which had for object the election of the Queen of May. He had met with violent opposition from a faction of ale-drinkers, who were in favour of a bouncing barmaid, the daughter of the innkeeper ; but he had been too strongly backed not to carry his point, though it shows that these rural crowns, like all others, are objects of great ambition and heart-burning. I am told that Master Simon takes great interest, though in an underhand way, in the election of these May-Day Queens, and that the chaplet is generally secured for some rustic beauty that has found favour in his eyes. In the

course of the day there were various games of strength and agility on the green, at which a knot of village veterans presided, as judges of the lists. Among those I perceived that Ready-Money Jack took the lead, looking with a learned and critical eye on the merits of the different candidates; and though he was very laconic, and sometimes merely expressed himself by a nod, yet it was evident that his opinions far outweighed those of the most loquacious.

Young Jack Tibbets was the hero of the day,
and carried off most of the prizes, though in some
of the feats of agility he was rivalled by the
"prodigal son," who appeared much in his element
on this occasion ; but his most formidable com-
petitor was the notorious gipsy, the redoubtable
"Starlight Tom." I was rejoiced at having an
opportunity of seeing this "minion of the moon"
in broad daylight. I found him a tall, swarthy,
good-looking fellow, with a lofty air, something
like what I have seen in an Indian chieftain ; and
with a certain lounging, easy, and almost graceful
carriage, which I have often remarked in beings
of the lazzaroni order, that lead an idle, loitering
life, and have a gentleman-like contempt of
labour.

Master Simon and the old general reconnoitred
the ground together, and indulged a vast deal of
harmless raking among the buxom country girls.
Master Simon would give some of them a kiss on
meeting with them, and would ask after their
sisters, for he is acquainted with most of the
farmers' families. Sometimes he would whisper,
and affect to talk mischievously with them, and, if
bantered on the subject, would turn it off with a

laugh, though it was evident he liked to be suspected of being a gay Lothario amongst them.

He had much to say to the farmers about their
farms, and seemed to know all their horses by
name. There was an old fellow, with a round,
ruddy face, and a night-cap under his hat, the
village wit, who took several occasions to crack a
joke with him in the hearing of his companions,
to whom he would turn and wink hard when
Master Simon had passed.

The harmony of the day, however, had nearly
at one time been interrupted by the appearance of
the radical on the ground, with two or three of his
disciples. He soon got engaged in argument in
the very thick of the throng, above which I could
hear his voice, and now and then see his meagre
hand, half a mile out of the sleeve, elevated in the
air in violent gesticulation, and flourishing a
pamphlet by way of truncheon. He was decrying
these idle nonsensical amusements in times of
public distress, when it was every one's business
to think of other matters, and to be miserable.
The honest village logicians could make no stand
against him, especially as he was seconded by his
proselytes; when, to their great joy, Master

Simon and the general came drifting down into
the field of action. I saw that Master Simon
was for making off, as soon as he found himself in
the neighbourhood of this fireship ; but the general
was too loyal to suffer such talk in his hearing,
and thought, no doubt, that a look and a word
from a gentleman would be sufficient to shut up
so shabby an orator. The latter, however, was no
respecter of persons, but rather seemed to exult in
having such important antagonists. He talked
with greater volubility than ever, and soon drowned
them with declamation on the subject of taxes,
poor's rates, and the national debt. Master Simon
endeavoured to brush along in his usual excursive
manner, which had always answered amazingly
well with the villagers ; but the radical was one of
those pestilent fellows that pin a man down to
facts, and, indeed, he had two or three pamphlets
in his pocket, to support everything he advanced
by printed documents. The general, too, found
himself betrayed into a more serious action than
his dignity could brook, and looked like a mighty
Dutch Indiaman grievously peppered by a petty
privateer. It was in vain that he swelled and
looked big, and talked large, and endeavoured to

make up by pomp of manner for poverty of matter;
every home-thrust of the radical made him wheeze
like a bellows, and seemed to let a volume of wind
out of him.   In a word, the two worthies from the
Hall were completely dumbfounded, and this, too,
in the presence of several of Master Simon's
staunch admirers, who had always looked up to
him as infallible.   I do not know how he and the
general would have managed to draw their forces
decently from the field, had there not been a match

at grinning through a horse-collar announced, whereupon the radical retired with great expression of contempt, and as soon as his back was turned, the argument was carried against him all hollow.

"Did you ever hear such a pack of stuff, general?" said Master Simon; "there's no talking with one of these chaps when he once gets that confounded Cobbett in his head."

"S'blood, sir!" said the general, wiping his forehead, "such fellows ought all to be transported!"

In the latter part of the day the ladies from the Hall paid a visit to the green. The fair Julia made her appearance, leaning on her lover's arm, and looking extremely pale and interesting. As she is a great favourite in the village, where she has been known from childhood, and as her late accident had been much talked about, the sight of her caused very manifest delight, and some of the old women of the village blessed her sweet face as she passed.

While they were walking about, I noticed the schoolmaster in earnest conversation with the young girl that represented the Queen of May, evidently endeavouring to spirit her up to some

formidable undertaking.   At length, as the party
from the Hall approached her bower, she came
forth, faltering at every step, until she reached the
spot where the fair Julia stood between her lover
and Lady Lillycraft.   The little Queen then
took the chaplet of flowers from her head, and
attempted to put it on that of the bride elect; but
the confusion of both was so great, that the wreath

would have fallen to the ground, had not the officer
caught it, and, laughing, placed it upon the blush-

ing brows of his mistress.   There was something
charming in the very embarrassment of these two
young creatures, both so beautiful, yet so different
in their kinds of beauty.   Master Simon told me,
afterwards, that the Queen of May was to have
spoken a few verses which the schoolmaster had
written for her; but that she had neither wit
to understand, nor memory to recollect them.
" Besides," added he, " between you and I, she
murders the king's English abominably; so she
has acted the part of a wise woman in holding her
tongue, and trusting to her pretty face."

Among the other characters from the Hall
was Mrs. Hannah, my lady Lillycraft's gentlewoman : to my surprise she was escorted by old
Christy the huntsman, and followed by his ghost
of a greyhound; but I find they are very old
acquaintances, being drawn together from some
sympathy of disposition.   Mrs. Hannah moved
about with starched dignity among the rustics,
who drew back from her with more awe than they
did from her mistress.   Her mouth seemed shut
as with a clasp ; excepting that I now and then
heard the word "fellows!" escape from between her
lips, as she got accidentally jostled in the crowd.

But there was one other heart present that did not enter into the merriment of the scene, which was that of the simple Phœbe Wilkins, the housekeeper's niece. The poor girl has continued to pine and whine for some time past, in consequence of the obstinate coldness of her lover; never was a little flirtation more severely punished. She appeared this day on the green, gallanted by a smart servant out of livery, and had evidently resolved to try the hazardous experiment of awakening the jealousy of her lover. She was dressed in her very best; affected an air of great gaiety: talked loud and girlishly, and laughed when there was nothing to laugh at. There was, however, an aching, heavy heart, in the poor baggage's bosom, in spite of all her levity. Her eye turned every now and then in quest of her reckless lover, and her cheek grew pale, and her fictitious gaiety vanished, on seeing him paying his rustic homage to the little May-day Queen.

My attention was now diverted by a fresh stir and bustle. Music was heard from a distance; a banner was seen advancing up the road, preceded by a rustic band playing something like a march, and followed by a sturdy throng of country

"A complete tumult ensued."—PAGE 237.

lads, the chivalry of a neighbouring and rival village.

No sooner had they reached the green than they challenged the heroes of the day to new trials of strength and activity. Several gymnastic contests ensued for the honour of the respective villages. In the course of these exercises, young Tibbets and the champion of the adverse party had an obstinate match at wrestling. They tugged, and strained, and panted, without either getting the mastery, until both came to the ground, and rolled upon the green. Just then the disconsolate Phœbe came by. She saw her recreant lover in fierce contest, as she thought, and in danger. In a moment pride, pique, and coquetry were forgotten; she rushed into the ring, seized upon the rival champion by the hair, and was on the point of wreaking on him her puny vengeance, when a buxom, strapping, country lass, the sweetheart of the prostrate swain, pounced upon her like a hawk, and would have stripped her of her fine plumage in a twinkling, had she also not been seized in her turn.

A complete tumult ensued. The chivalry of the two villages became embroiled. Blows began to be dealt, and sticks to be flourished. Phœbe was carried off from the field in hysterics. In vain did the sages of the village interfere. The sententious apothecary endeavoured to pour the soothing oil of his philosophy upon this tempestuous sea of passion, but was tumbled into the dust. Slingsby, the pedagogue, who is a great lover of peace, went into the middle of the throng, as marshal of the day, to put an end to the commotion, but was rent in twain, and came out with his garment hanging in two strips from his shoulders; upon which the prodigal son dashed in with fury to revenge the insult which his patron had sustained. The tumult thickened; I caught glimpses of the jockey-cap of old Christy, like the helmet of a chieftain, bobbing about in the midst of the scuffle; while Mrs. Hannah, separated from her doughty protector, was squalling and striking at right and left with a faded parasol; being tossed and tousled about by the crowd in such wise as never happened to maiden gentlewoman before.

At length I beheld old Ready-Money Jack making his way into the very thickest of the throng; tearing it, as it were, apart, and enforcing peace *vi et armis*. It was surprising to see the sudden quiet that ensued. The storm settled down at once into tranquillity. The parties, having no real grounds of hostility, were readily pacified, and in fact were a little at a loss to know why and how they had got by the ears. Slingsby was speedily stitched together again by his friend the tailor, and resumed his usual good humour. Mrs. Hannah drew on one side to plume her rumpled feathers; and old Christy, having repaired his damages, took her under his arm, and they swept

back again to the Hall, ten times more bitter against mankind than ever.

The Tibbets family alone seemed slow in recovering from the agitation of the scene. Young Jack was evidently very much moved by the heroism of the unlucky Phœbe. His mother, who had been summoned to the field of action by news of the affray, was in a sad panic, and had need of all her management to keep him from following his mistress, and coming to a perfect reconciliation.

What heightened the alarm and perplexity of the good managing dame was, that the matter had roused the slow apprehension of old Ready-Money himself; who was very much struck by the intrepid interference of so pretty and delicate a girl, and was sadly puzzled to understand the meaning of the violent agitation in his family.

When all this came to the ears of the squire, he was grievously scandalised that his May-day fête should have been disgraced by such a brawl. He ordered Phœbe to appear before him; but the girl was so frightened and distressed, that she came sobbing and trembling, and, at the first question he asked, fell again into hysterics. Lady Lillycraft, who had understood that there was an affair of the heart at the bottom of this distress, immediately took the girl into great favour and protection, and made her peace with the squire. This was the only thing that disturbed the harmony of the day, if we except the discomfiture of Master Simon and the general by the radical. Upon the whole, therefore, the squire had very fair reason to be satisfied that he had rode his hobby throughout the day without any other molestation.

The reader, learned in these matters, will perceive that all this was but a faint shadow of the once gay and fanciful rites of May. The peasantry have lost the proper feeling for these rites, and have grown almost as strange to them as the boors of La Mancha were to the customs of chivalry in the days of the valorous Don Quixote. Indeed, I considered it a proof of the discretion with which the squire rides his hobby, that he had not pushed the thing any farther, nor attempted to revive many obsolete usages of the day, which, in the present matter-of-fact times, would appear affected and absurd. I must say, though I do it under the rose, the general brawl in which this festival had nearly terminated, has made me doubt

R

whether these rural customs of the good old times were always so very loving and innocent as we are apt to fancy them ; and whether the peasantry in those times were really so Arcadian as they have been fondly represented.   I begin to fear

> ———— " Those days were never ; airy dreams
> Sat for the picture, and the poet's hand,
> Imparting substance to an empty shade,
> Imposed a gay delirium for a truth.
> Grant it ; I still must envy them an age
> That favoured such a dream."

THE CULPRIT.

From fire, from water, and all things amiss,
Deliver the house of an honest justice.
THE WIDOW.

THE serenity of the Hall has been suddenly interrupted by a very important occurrence. In the
course of this morning a posse of villagers was
seen trooping up the avenue, with boys shouting
in advance. As it drew near, we perceived Ready-
Money Jack Tibbets striding along, wielding his
cudgel in one hand, and with the other grasping
the collar of a tall fellow, whom, on still nearer
approach, we recognised for the redoubtable gipsy
hero, Starlight Tom. He was now, however,

completely cowed and crestfallen, and his courage
seemed to have quailed in the iron gripe of the
lion-hearted Jack.

The whole gang of gipsy women and children
came draggling in the rear; some in tears, others
making a violent clamour about the ears of old
Ready-Money, who, however, trudged on in silence
with his prey, heeding their abuse as little as a
hawk that has pounced upon a barn-door hero
regards the outcries and cacklings of his whole
feathered seraglio.

He had passed through the village on his way
to the Hall, and of course had made a great sensation in that most excitable place, where every
event is a matter of gaze and gossip. The report
flew like wildfire that Starlight Tom was in cus-
tody. The ale-drinkers forthwith abandoned the
tap-room; Slingsby's school broke loose, and
master and boys swelled the tide that came
rolling at the heels of old Ready-Money and his
captive.

The uproar increased as they approached the
Hall; it aroused the whole garrison of dogs, and
the crew of hangers-on. The great mastiff barked
from the dog-house; the staghound, and the grey-

hound, and the spaniel, issued barking from the Hall door, and my Lady Lillycraft's little dogs ramped and barked from the parlour window. I remarked, however, that the gipsy dogs made no reply to all these menaces and insults, but crept close to the gang, looking round with a guilty,

poaching air, and now and then glancing up a dubious eye to their owners ; which shows that the moral dignity, even of dogs, may be ruined by bad company !

When the throng reached the front of the house, they were brought to a halt by a kind of advanced guard, composed of old Christy, the gamekeeper, and two or three servants of the house, who had been brought out by the noise.

The common herd of the village fell back with respect; the boys were driven back by Christy and his compeers; while Ready-Money Jack maintained his ground and his hold of the prisoner, and was surrounded by the tailor, the schoolmaster, and several other dignitaries of the village, and by the clamorous brood of gipsies, who were neither to be silenced nor intimidated.

By this time the whole household were brought to the doors and windows, and the squire to the portal. An audience was demanded by Ready-Money Jack, who had detected the prisoner in the very act of sheep-stealing on his domains, and had borne him off to be examined before the squire, who is in the commission of the peace.

A kind of tribunal was immediately held in the servants' hall, a large chamber with a stone floor and a long table in the centre, at one end of which, just under an enormous clock, was placed the squire's chair of justice, while Master Simon took his place at the table as clerk of the court. An attempt had been made by old Christy to keep out the gipsy gang, but in vain; and they, with

"A kind of tribunal was immediately held in the servants' hall."—PAGE 246.

the village worthies, and the household, half filled the hall. The old housekeeper and the butler were in a panic at this dangerous irruption. They hurried away all the valuable things and portable articles that were at hand, and even kept a dragon watch on the gipsies, lest they should carry off the house clock or the deal table.

Old Christy, and his faithful coadjutor, the gamekeeper, acted as constables to guard the prisoner, triumphing in having at last got this terrible offender in their clutches. Indeed I am inclined to think the old man bore some peevish recollection of having been handled rather roughly by the gipsy in the chance-medley affair of May-day.

Silence was now commanded by Master Simon ; but it was difficult to be enforced in such a motley assemblage. There was a continued snarling and yelping of dogs, and, as fast as it was quelled in one corner, it broke out in another. The poor gipsy curs, who, like errant thieves, could not hold up their heads in an honest house, were worried and insulted by the gentleman dogs of the establishment, without offering to make

resistance; the very curs of my Lady Lillycraft
bullied them with impunity.

The examination was conducted with great
mildness and indulgence by the squire, partly from
the kindness of his nature, and partly, I suspect,
because his heart yearned towards the culprit, who
had found great favour in his eyes, as I have
already observed, from the skill he had at various
times displayed in archery, morris-dancing, and
other obsolete accomplishments.   Proofs, however,
were too strong.   Ready-Money Jack told his
story in a straightforward independent way,
nothing daunted by the presence in which he
found himself.   He had suffered from various
depredations on his sheep-fold and poultry-yard,
and had at length kept watch, and caught the
delinquent in the very act of making off with a
sheep on his shoulders.

Tibbets was repeatedly interrupted, in the
course of his testimony, by the culprit's mother, a
furious old beldame, with an insufferable tongue,
and who, in fact, was several times kept, with
some difficulty, from flying at him tooth and nail.
The wife, too, of the prisoner, whom I am told he
does not beat above half a dozen times a week,

completely interested Lady Lillycraft in her husband's behalf, by her tears and supplications; and several of the other gipsy women were awakening strong sympathy among the young girls and maid-servants in the background. The pretty, black-eyed gipsy girl, whom I have mentioned on a former occasion as the sibyl that read the fortunes of the general, endeavoured to wheedle that doughty warrior into their interests, and even made some approaches to her old acquaintance, Master Simon; but was repelled by the latter with all the dignity of office, having assumed a look of gravity and importance suitable to the occasion.

I was a little surprised, at first, to find honest Slingsby, the schoolmaster, rather opposed to his old crony Tibbets, and coming forwards as a kind of advocate for the accused. It seems that he had taken compassion on the forlorn fortunes of Starlight Tom, and had been trying his eloquence in his favour the whole way from the village, but without effect. During the examination of Ready-Money Jack, Slingsby had stood like "dejected Pity at his side," seeking every now and then, by a soft word, to soothe any exacerbation of his ire, or to qualify any harsh expression. He now ventured to make a few observations to the squire in palliation of the delinquent's offence; but poor Slingsby spoke more from the heart than the head, and was evidently actuated merely by a general sympathy for every poor devil in trouble, and a liberal toleration for all kinds of vagabond existence.

The ladies, too, large and small, with the kind-heartedness of their sex, were zealous on the side of mercy, and interceded strenuously with the squire; insomuch that the prisoner, finding himself unexpectedly surrounded by active friends, once more reared his crest, and seemed disposed for a time to put on the air of injured innocence. The squire, however, with all his benevolence of heart, and his lurking weakness towards the prisoner, was too conscientious to swerve from the strict path of justice. There was abundant concurrent testimony that made the proof of guilt incontrovertible, and Starlight Tom's mittimus was made out accordingly.

The sympathy of the ladies was now greater than ever; they even made some attempts to mollify the ire of Ready-Money Jack; but that

sturdy potentate had been too much incensed by
the repeated incursions that had been made into
his territories by the predatory band of Starlight
Tom, and he was resolved, he said, to drive the
"varmint reptiles" out of the neighbourhood.
To avoid all further importunities, as soon as the
mittimus was made out, he girded up his loins,
and strode back to his seat of empire, accompanied by his interceding friend, Slingsby, and
followed by a detachment of the gipsy gang, who
hung on his rear, assailing him with mingled
prayers and execrations.

The question now was, how to dispose of the
prisoner ; a matter of great moment in this peace-
ful establishment, where so formidable a character
as Starlight Tom was like a hawk entrapped in a
dovecot. As the hubbub and examination had
occupied a considerable time, it was too late in
the day to send him to the county prison, and
that of the village was sadly out of repair from
long want of occupation. Old Christy, who took
great interest in the affair, proposed that the
culprit should be committed for the night to an
upper loft of a kind of tower in one of the out-
houses, where he and the gamekeeper would

mount guard.   After much deliberation this
measure was adopted; the premises in question
were examined and made secure, and Christy and
his trusty ally, the one armed with a fowling-piece,
the other with an ancient blunderbuss, turned out
as sentries to keep watch over this donjon-keep.

Such is the momentous affair that has just
taken place, and it is an event of too great moment
in this quiet little world, not to turn it completely

topsy-turvy. Labour is at a stand. The house has been a scene of confusion the whole evening. It has been beleaguered by gipsy women, with their children on their backs, wailing and lamenting; while the old virago of a mother has cruised up and down the lawn in front, shaking her head and muttering to herself, or now and then breaking out into a paroxysm of rage, brandishing her fist at the Hall, and denouncing ill-luck upon Ready-Money Jack, and even upon the squire himself.

Lady Lillycraft has given repeated audiences to the culprit's weeping wife, at the Hall door; and the servant-maids have stolen out to confer with the gipsy women under the trees. As to the little ladies of the family, they are all outrageous at Ready-Money Jack, whom they look upon in the light of a tyrannical giant of fairy tale. Phœbe Wilkins, contrary to her usual nature, is the only one that is pitiless in the affair. She thinks Mr. Tibbets quite in the right; and thinks the gipsies deserve to be punished severely for meddling with the sheep of the Tibbetses.

In the meantime the females of the family

have evinced all the provident kindness of the
sex, ever ready to soothe and succour the distressed,
right or wrong.   Lady Lillycraft has had a mattress
taken to the out-house, and comforts and delicacies
of all kinds have been taken to the prisoner ; even
the little girls have sent their cakes and sweet-
meats ; so that, I'll warrant, the vagabond has
never fared so well in his life before.   Old
Christy, it is true, looks upon everything with a
wary eye ; struts about with his blunderbuss with
the air of a veteran campaigner, and will hardly
allow himself to be spoken to.   The gipsy women
dare not come within gunshot, and every tatter-
demallion of a boy has been frightened from the
park.   The old fellow is determined to lodge
Starlight Tom in prison with his own hands ;
 nd hopes, he says, to see one of the poaching
crew made an example of.

I doubt, after all, whether the worthy squire is
not the greatest sufferer in the whole affair.   His
honourable sense of duty obliges him to be rigid,
but the overflowing kindness of his nature makes
this a grievous trial to him.

He is not accustomed to have such demands
upon his justice in his truly patriarchal domain ;

and it wounds his benevolent spirit, that, while prosperity and happiness are flowing in thus bounteously upon him, he should have to inflict misery upon a fellow-being.

He has been troubled and cast down the whole evening : took leave of the family, on going to bed, with a sigh, instead of his usual hearty and affectionate tone, and will, in all probability, have a far more sleepless night than his prisoner. Indeed this unlucky affair has cast a damp upon the whole household, as there appears to be an universal opinion that the unlucky culprit will come to the gallows.

Morning.—The clouds of last evening are all blown over. A load has been taken from the squire's heart, and every face is once more in smiles. The gamekeeper made his appearance at an early hour, completely shamefaced and crest-fallen. Starlight Tom had made his escape in the night; how he had got out of the loft no one could tell; the devil, they think, must have assisted him. Old Christy was so mortified that he would not show his face, but had shut himself up in his stronghold at the dog-kennel, and would not be spoken with. What has particu-

larly relieved the squire is, that there is very
little likelihood of the culprit's being retaken,
having gone off on one of the old gentleman's
best hunters.

LOVERS' TROUBLES.

The poor soul sat singing by a sycamore tree.
    Sing all a green willow ;
Her hand on her bosom, her head on her knee,
    Sing willow, willow, willow ;
Sing all a green willow must be my garland.

OLD SONG.

THE fair Julia having nearly recovered from the effects of her hawking disaster, it begins to be thought high time to appoint a day for the wedding. As every domestic event in a venerable and aristocratic family connection like this is a matter of moment, the fixing upon this important day has, of course, given rise to much conference and debate.

Some slight difficulties and demurs have lately sprung up, originating in the peculiar humours that are prevalent at the Hall. Thus, I have overheard a very solemn consultation between Lady Lillycraft, the parson, and Master Simon, as to whether the marriage ought not to be postponed until the coming month.

With all the charms of the flowery month of May, there is, I find, an ancient prejudice against it as a marrying month. An old proverb says, "To wed in May, is to wed poverty." Now, as Lady Lillycraft is very much given to believe in lucky and unlucky times and seasons, and indeed is very superstitious on all points relating to the tender passion, this old proverb seems to have taken great hold upon her mind. She recollects two or three instances in her own knowledge of matches that took place in this month, and proved very unfortunate. Indeed, an own cousin of hers, who married on a May-day, lost her husband by a fall from his horse, after they had lived happily together for twenty years.

The parson appeared to give great weight to

her ladyship's objections, and acknowledged the existence of a prejudice of the kind, not merely confined to modern times, but prevalent likewise among the ancients. In confirmation of this, he quoted a passage from Ovid, which had a great effect on Lady Lillycraft, being given in a language which she did not understand. Even Master Simon was staggered by it; for he listened with a puzzled air, and then, shaking his head, sagaciously observed that Ovid was certainly a very wise man.

From this sage conference I likewise gathered several other important pieces of information relative to weddings; such as that if two were celebrated in the same church on the same day, the first would be happy, the second unfortunate. If, on going to church, the bridal party should meet the funeral of a female, it was an omen that the bride would die first; if of a male, the bridegroom. If the newly-married couple were to dance together on their wedding-day, the wife would thenceforth rule the roast; with many other curious and unquestionable facts of the same nature, all which made me ponder more than ever upon the perils which surround this happy state, and the thoughtless ignorance of mortals as to the awful risks they run in entering upon it.   I abstain, however, from enlarging upon this topic, having no inclination to promote the increase of bachelors.

Notwithstanding the due weight which the squire gives to traditional saws and ancient opinions, yet I am happy to find that he makes a firm stand for the credit of this loving month, and brings to his aid a whole legion of poetical authorities; all which, I presume, have been conclusive with the young couple, as I understand they are perfectly willing to marry in May, and abide the consequences.   In a few days, therefore, the wedding is to take place, and the Hall is in a buzz of anticipation.   The housekeeper is bustling about from morning till night, with a look full of business and importance, having a thousand arrangements to make, the squire intending to keep open house on the occasion; and as to the housemaids, you cannot look one of them in the face, but the rogue begins to colour up and simper.

While, however, this leading love affair is going on with a tranquillity quite inconsistent with the rules of romance, I cannot say that the underplots are equally propitious.   The "opening bud

of love" between the general and Lady Lillycraft
seems to have experienced some blight in the
course of this genial season. I do not think the
general has ever been able to retrieve the ground
he lost when he fell asleep during the captain's
story. Indeed, Master Simon thinks his case
is completely desperate, her ladyship having
determined that he is quite destitute of sentiment.

The season has been equally unpropitious to
the love-lorn Phœbe Wilkins. I fear the reader
will be impatient at having this humble amour so
often alluded to ; but I confess I am apt to take a
great interest in the love troubles of simple girls
of this class. Few people have an idea of the
world of care and perplexity that these poor
damsels have in managing the affairs of the heart.

We talk and write about the tender passion ;
we give it all the colourings of sentiment and
romance, and lay the scene of its influence in high
life ; but, after all, I doubt whether its sway is not
more absolute among females of a humbler sphere.
How often, could we but look into the heart,
should we find the sentiment throbbing in all its
violence, in the bosom of the poor lady's maid,
rather than in that of the brilliant beauty she is

decking out for conquest; whose brain is probably bewildered with beaux, ball-rooms, and wax-light chandeliers.

With these humble beings love is an honest, engrossing concern. They have no ideas of settlements, establishments, equipages, and pin-money. The heart—the heart—is all-in-all with them, poor things! There is seldom one of them but has her love cares, and love secrets; her doubts, and hopes, and fears, equal to those of any heroine of romance, and ten times as sincere. And then, too, there is her secret hoard of love documents;

—the broken sixpence, the gilded brooch, the lock of hair, the unintelligible love scrawl, all treasured up in her box of Sunday finery, for private contemplation.

How many crosses and trials is she exposed to from some lynx-eyed dame, or staid old vestal of a mistress, who keeps a dragon watch over her virtue, and scouts the lover from the door! But then how sweet are the little love scenes, snatched at distant intervals of holiday, fondly dwelt on through many a long day of household labour and confinement! If in the country, it is the dance at the fair or wake, the interview in the church-yard after service, or the evening stroll in the green lane. If in town, it is perhaps merely a stolen moment of delicious talk between the bars of the area, fearful every instant of being seen ; and then, how lightly will the simple creature carol all day afterwards at her labour!

Poor baggage! after all her crosses and difficulties, when she marries, what is it but to exchange a life of comparative ease and comfort for one of toil and uncertainty ? Perhaps, too, the lover, for whom, in the fondness of her nature, she has committed herself to fortune's freaks, turns out a worthless churl, the dissolute, hard-hearted husband of low life ; who, taking to the alehouse, leaves her to a cheerless home, to labour, penury, and child-bearing.

When I see poor Phœbe going about with drooping eye, and her head hanging "all o' one side," I cannot help calling to mind the pathetic little picture drawn by Desdemona :—

> " My mother had a maid, called Barbara ;
> She was in love ; and he she loved proved mad
> And did forsake her ; she had a song of willow,
> An old thing 'twas ; but it express'd her fortune,
> And she died singing it."

I hope, however, that a better lot is in reserve for Phœbe Wilkins, and that she may yet "rule the roast," in the ancient empire of the Tibbetses ! She is not fit to battle with hard hearts or hard times. She was, I am told, the pet of her poor mother, who was proud of the beauty of her child, and brought her up more tenderly than a village girl ought to be ; and ever since she has been left an orphan, the good ladies at the Hall have completed the softening and spoiling of her.

I have recently observed her holding long con-
ferences in the churchyard, and up and down one
of the lanes near the village, with Slingsby the
schoolmaster. I at first thought the pedagogue
might be touched with the tender malady so prevalent in these parts of late; but I did him in-
justice. Honest Slingsby, it seems, was a friend
and crony of her late father, the parish clerk;
and is on intimate terms with the Tibbets family.
Prompted, therefore, by his good-will towards all
parties, and secretly instigated, perhaps, by the

managing dame Tibbets, he has undertaken to
talk with Phœbe upon the subject.　He gives her,
however, but little encouragement.　Slingsby has
a formidable opinion of the aristocratical feeling of
old Ready-Money, and thinks, if Phœbe were even
to make the matter up with the son, she would
find the father totally hostile to the match.　The
poor damsel, therefore, is reduced almost to
despair ; and Slingsby, who is too good-natured
not to sympathise in her distress, has advised her
to give up all thoughts of young Jack, and has
promised as a substitute his learned coadjutor, the
prodigal son.　He has even, in the fulness of his
heart, offered to give up the school-house to them,
though it would leave him once more adrift in the
wide world.

THE WEDDING.

No more, no more, much honour aye betide
The lofty bridegroom, and the lovely bride ;
That all of their succeeding days may say,
Each day appears like to a wedding day.

Braithwaite.

Notwithstanding the doubts and demurs of Lady
Lillycraft, and all the grave objections that were
conjured up against the month of May, yet the
Wedding has at length happily taken place. It
was celebrated at the village church in presence of
a numerous company of relatives and friends, and
many of the tenantry. The squire must needs
have something of the old ceremonies observed on

the occasion ; so at the gate of the churchyard, several little girls of the village, dressed in white, were in readiness with baskets of flowers, which they strewed before the bride ; and the butler bore before her the bride-cup, a great silver embossed bowl, one of the family reliques from the days of the hard drinkers. This was filled with rich wine, and decorated with a branch of rosemary, tied with gay ribands, according to ancient custom.

"Happy is the bride that the sun shines on," says the old proverb ; and it was as sunny and auspicious a morning as heart could wish. The bride looked uncommonly beautiful ; but, in fact, what woman does not look interesting on her wedding-day? I know no sight more charming and touching than that of a young and timid bride, in her robes of virgin white, led up trembling to the altar. When I thus behold a lovely girl, in the tenderness of her years, forsaking the house of her fathers and the home of her childhood, and, with the implicit, confiding, and the sweet self-abandonment which belong to woman, giving up all the world for the man of her choice ; when I hear her, in the good old language of the ritual, yielding herself to him "for better for worse, for richer for poorer, in sickness and in health ; to love, honour, and obey, till death us do part," it brings to my mind the beautiful and affecting self-devotion of Ruth :—" Whither thou goest I will go, and where thou lodgest I will lodge ; thy people shall be my people, and thy God my God."

The fair Julia was supported on the trying occasion by Lady Lillycraft, whose heart was overflowing with its wonted sympathy in all matters of love and matrimony. As the bride approached the altar, her face would be one moment covered with blushes, and the next deadly pale ; and she seemed almost ready to shrink from sight among her female companions.

I do not know what it is that makes every one serious, and, as it were, awestruck at a marriage ceremony, which is generally considered as an occasion of festivity and rejoicing. As the ceremony was performing, I observed many a rosy face among the country girls turn pale, and I did not see a smile throughout the church. The young ladies from the Hall were almost as much frightened as if it had been their own case, and stole many a look of sympathy at their trembling companion. A tear stood in the eye of the sensitive Lady Lillycraft; and as to Phœbe Wilkins, who was present, she absolutely wept and sobbed aloud; but it is hard to tell half the time what these fond, foolish creatures are crying about.

The captain, too, though naturally gay and unconcerned, was much agitated on the occasion, and, in attempting to put the ring upon the bride's finger, dropped it on the floor; which Lady Lillycraft has since assured me is a very lucky omen. Even Master Simon had lost his usual vivacity, and had assumed a most whimsically solemn face, which he is apt to do on all occasions of ceremony. He had much whispering with the parson and parish-clerk, for he is always a busy personage in the scene; and he echoed the clerk's amen with a solemnity and devotion that edified the whole assemblage.

The moment, however, that the ceremony was over, the transition was magical. The bride-cup was passed round, according to ancient usage, for the company to drink to a happy union; every one's feelings seemed to break forth from restraint; Master Simon had a world of bachelor pleasantries to utter, and as to the gallant general, he

"The villagers gathered in the churchyard to cheer the happy couple."—PAGE 271.

bowed and cooed about the dulcet Lady Lillycraft,
like a mighty cock pigeon about his dame.

The villagers gathered in the churchyard to
cheer the happy couple as they left the church;
and the musical tailor had marshalled his band, and
set up a hideous discord, as the blushing and smil-
ing bride passed through a lane of honest peasantry
to her carriage. The children shouted and threw
up their hats; the bells rung a merry peal that set
all the crows and rooks flying and cawing about
the air, and threatened to bring down the battle-
ments of the old tower; and there was a continual
popping off of rusty firelocks from every part of
the neighbourhood.

The prodigal son distinguished himself on the
occasion, having hoisted a flag on the top of the
school-house, and kept the village in a hubbub from
sunrise with the sound of drum, and fife, and pandean pipe; in which species of music several of
his scholars are making wonderful proficiency. In
his great zeal, however, he had nearly done mischief; for, on returning from church, the horses
of the bride's carriage took fright from the discharge of a row of old gun-barrels, which he
had mounted as a park of artillery in front of the

school-house, to give the captain a military salute
as he passed.

The day passed off with great rustic rejoicings.
Tables were spread under the trees in the park,
where all the peasantry of the neighbourhood were
regaled with roast beef and plum-pudding, and
oceans of ale. Ready-Money Jack presided at one
of the tables, and became so full of good cheer, as
to unbend from his usual gravity, to sing a song
out of all tune, and give two or three shouts of
laughter, that almost electrified his neighbours,
like so many peals of thunder. The schoolmaster

and the apothecary vied with each other in making speeches over their liquor ; and there were occasional glees and musical performances by the village band, that must have frightened every faun and dryad from the park. Even old Christy, who had got on a new dress, from top to toe, and shone in all the splendour of bright leather breeches, and an enormous wedding favour in his cap, forgot his usual crustiness, became inspired by wine and wassail, and absolutely danced a hornpipe on one of the tables, with all the grace and agility of a mannikin hung upon wires.

Equal gaiety reigned within doors, where a large party of friends were entertained. Every one laughed at his own pleasantry, without attending to that of his neighbours. Loads of bride-cake were distributed. The young ladies were all busy in passing morsels of it through the wedding ring to dream on, and I myself assisted a fine little boarding-school girl in putting up a quantity for her companions, which I have no doubt will set all the little heads in the school gadding, for a week at least.

After dinner all the company, great and small, gentle and simple, abandoned themselves to the

T

dance : not the modern quadrille, with its graceful
gravity, but the merry, social, old country dance ;
the true dance, as the squire says, for a wedding
occasion ; as it sets all the world jigging in couples,
hand in hand, and makes every eye and every
heart dance merrily to the music.   According to
frank old usage, the gentlefolks of the Hall
mingled, for a time, in the dance of the peasantry,
who had a great tent erected for a ball-room ; and
I think I never saw Master Simon more in his
element than when figuring about among his

rustic admirers, as master of the ceremonies; and, with a mingled air of protection and gallantry, leading out the quondam Queen of May—all blushing at the signal honour conferred upon her.

In the evening, the whole village was illuminated, excepting the house of the radical, who has not shown his face during the rejoicings. There was a display of fireworks at the school-house, got up by the prodigal son, which had wellnigh set fire to the building. The squire is so much pleased with the extraordinary services of this last-mentioned worthy, that he talks of enrolling him in his list of valuable retainers, and promoting him to some important post on the estate; peradventure to be falconer, if the hawks can ever be brought into proper training.

There is a well-known old proverb that says, "one wedding makes many"—or something to the same purpose; and I should not be surprised if it holds good in the present instance. I have seen several flirtations among the young people that have been brought together on this occasion; and a great deal of strolling about in pairs, among the retired walks and blossoming shrubberies of the old garden; and if groves were really given to whispering, as poets would fain make us believe, Heaven knows what love-tales the grave-looking old trees about this venerable country-seat might blab to the world. The general, too, has waxed very zealous in his devotions within the last few days, as the time of her ladyship's departure approaches. I observed him casting many a tender look at her during the wedding dinner, while the courses were changing; though he was always liable to be interrupted in his adoration by the appearance of any new delicacy. The general, in fact, has arrived at that time of life when the heart and the stomach maintain a kind of balance of power; and when a man is apt to be perplexed in his affections between a fine woman and a truffled turkey. Her ladyship was certainly rivalled through the whole of the first course by a dish of stewed carp; and there was one glance, which was evidently intended to be a point-blank shot at her heart, and could scarcely have failed to effect a practicable breach, had it not unluckily been diverted away to a tempting breast of lamb, in which it immediately produced a formidable incision.

Thus did the faithless general go on, coquetting during the whole dinner, and committing an infidelity with every new dish; until, in the end, he was so overpowered by the attentions he had paid to fish, flesh, and fowl; to pastry, jelly, cream, and blancmange, that he seemed to sink within himself : his eyes swam beneath their lids, and their fire was so much slackened, that he could no longer discharge a single glance that would reach across the table. Upon the whole, I fear the general ate himself into as much disgrace, at this memorable dinner, as I have seen him sleep himself into on a former occasion.

I am told, moreover, that young Jack Tibbets was so touched by the wedding ceremony, at which he was present, and so captivated by the sensibility of poor Phœbe Wilkins, who certainly looked all the better for her tears, that he had a reconciliation with her that very day, after dinner, in one of the groves of the park, and danced with her in the evening; to the complete confusion of all Dame Tibbets' domestic politics. I met them walking together in the park, shortly after the reconciliation must have taken place. Young Jack carried himself gaily and manfully; but Phœbe hung her head, blushing, as I approached. However, just as she passed me, and dropped a curtsy, I caught a shy

gleam of her eye from under her bonnet ; but it
was immediately cast down again.   I saw enough
in that single gleam, and in the involuntary smile
that dimpled about her rosy lips, to feel satisfied
that the little gipsy's heart was happy again.

What is more, Lady Lillycraft, with her usual
benevolence and zeal in all matters of this tender
nature, on hearing of the reconciliation of the

lovers, undertook the critical task of breaking the matter to Ready-Money Jack. She thought there was no time like the present, and attacked the sturdy old yeoman that very evening in the park, while his heart was yet lifted up with the squire's good cheer. Jack was a little surprised at being drawn aside by her ladyship, but was not to be flurried by such an honour : he was still more surprised by the nature of her communication, and by this first intelligence of an affair that had been passing under his eye. He listened, however, with his usual gravity, as her ladyship represented the advantages of the match, the good qualities of the girl, and the distress which she had lately suffered ; at length his eye began to kindle, and his hand to play with the head of his cudgel. Lady Lillycraft saw that something in the narrative had gone wrong, and hastened to mollify his rising ire by reiterating the soft-hearted Phœbe's merit and fidelity, and her great unhappiness, when old Ready-Money suddenly interrupted her by exclaiming, that if Jack did not marry the wench, he'd break every bone in his body ! The match, therefore, is considered a settled thing ; Dame Tibbets and the housekeeper have made friends, and drank tea together; and Phœbe has again recovered her good looks and good spirits, and is carolling from morning till night like a lark.

But the most whimsical caprice of Cupid is one that I should be almost afraid to mention, did I not know that I was writing for readers well acquainted in the waywardness of this most mischievous deity. The morning after the wedding, therefore, while Lady Lillycraft was making preparations for her departure, an audience was requested by her immaculate handmaid, Mrs. Hannah, who, with much priming of the mouth, and many maidenly hesitations, requested leave to stay behind, and that Lady Lillycraft would supply her place with some other servant. Her ladyship was astonished: "What! Hannah going to quit her, that had lived with her so long!"

"Why, one could not help it; one must settle in life some time or other."

The good lady was still lost in amazement; at length the secret was gasped from the dry lips of the maiden gentlewoman; "she had been some time thinking of changing her condition, and at length had given her word, last evening, to Mr. Christy, the huntsman.

How, or when, or where this singular courtship had been carried on, I have not been able to
learn; nor how she has been able, with the vinegar
of her disposition, to soften the stony heart of old
Nimrod; so, however, it is, and it has astonished
every one.   With all her ladyship's love of match-
making, this last fume of Hymen's torch has been
too much for her.   She has endeavoured to reason
with Mrs. Hannah, but all in vain; her mind was
made up, and she grew tart on the least contra-
diction.   Lady Lillycraft applied to the squire for

his interference. "She did not know what she should do without Mrs. Hannah, she had been used to have her about her so long a time."

The squire, on the contrary, rejoiced in the match, as relieving the good lady from a kind of toilet-tyrant, under whose sway she had suffered for years. Instead of thwarting the affair, therefore, he has given it his full countenance; and declares that he will set up the young couple in one of the best cottages on his estate. The approbation of the squire has been followed by that of the whole household; they all declare, that if ever matches are really made in heaven, this must have been; for that old Christy and Mrs. Hannah were as evidently formed to be linked together as ever were pepper-box and vinegar-cruet.

As soon as this matter was arranged, Lady Lillycraft took her leave of the family at the Hall; taking with her the captain and his blushing bride, who are to pass the honeymoon with her. Master Simon accompanied them on horseback, and indeed means to ride on ahead to make preparations. The general, who was fishing in vain for an invitation to her seat, handed her ladyship into her carriage with a heavy sigh; upon which his bosom friend, Master Simon, who was just mounting his horse, gave me a knowing wink, made an abominably wry face, and, leaning from his saddle, whispered loudly in my ear, " It won't do!" Then putting spurs to his horse, away he cantered off. The general stood for some time waving his hat after the carriage as it rolled down the avenue, until he was seized with a fit of sneezing, from exposing his head to the cool breeze. I observed that he returned rather thoughtfully to the house; whistling thoughtfully to himself, with his hands behind his back, and an exceedingly dubious air.

The company have now almost all taken their departure. I have determined to do the same to-morrow morning; and I hope my reader may not think that I have already lingered too long at the Hall. I have been tempted to do so, however, because I thought I had lit upon one of the retired places where there are yet some traces to be met with of old English character. A little while hence, and all these will probably have passed away. Ready-Money Jack will sleep with his fathers : the good squire, and all his peculiarities, will be buried in the neighbouring church. The old Hall will be modernised into a fashionable country-seat, or, peradventure, a manufactory. The park will be cut up into petty farms and kitchen-gardens. A daily coach will run through the village; it will become, like all other commonplace villages, thronged with coachmen, post-boys, tipplers, and politicians; and Christmas, May-day, and all the other hearty merry-makings of the "good old times" will be forgotten.

Editor's Note to the Facsimile Edition

The reader for quiet pleasure, surely the "Worthy Reader" Geoffrey Crayon customarily addressed in prefatory remarks, need not be as concerned, as is the "Literary Antiquary" just met, with the minutiae of bibliographical detail. Still, for completeness, it might well be noted that publisher Macmillan, in choosing the precise *Bracebridge Hall* to draw from in reprint, did not select Irving's own Author's Revised Edition (New York, 1849). Instead the 1877 volume, and thus the present SHR facsimile, apparently derive from a copy of the English edition of 1823, a "New Edition" published, like the London original of 1822, by the famous John Murray. Irving had reworked his text for this next occasion: witness the first appearance in "Bachelors" (present page 89, line 8) of the phrasing, "but, as Major Pendergast says, a married man. . . ." Irving later dropped the male chauvinist major here, but retained the barbed remark. There was, after all, no Mrs. Geoffrey Crayon to read it.

Old Christmas

from *The Sketch Book* by Washington Irving
illustrated by Randolph Caldecott

A Facsimile of the 1875 First Edition

Five timeless tales of an old-fashioned Christmas, with mistletoe, evergreens, the blazing Yule log, caroling, dancing, wine and wassail, and the festive Christmas dinner.

With the original 106 illustrations by Randolph Caldecott, noted nineteenth century artist and illustrator of children's books.

Bound in dark green cloth with Caldecott's original cover design die-stamped in gold, this facsimile reproduces as precisely as possible every aspect of the First Edition.

A new Introduction by Dr. Andrew B. Myers of Fordham University discusses the Irving-Caldecott collaboration and the enduring popularity of these stories for more than a century.

108 pages   106 illustrations   clothbound, $10.00

Rip Van Winkle & The Legend of Sleepy Hollow

by Washington Irving

illustrated by Felix O. C. Darley

The two most popular stories from Washington Irving's *Sketch Book*, with text from the Author's Revised Edition of 1848, reproductions of original manuscript pages from both stories, and twelve full-page illustrations by nineteenth century artist Felix O. C. Darley, illuminated in *full color*.

An Introduction by Professor Haskell Springer of the University of Kansas discusses the significance of the tales and Irving's importance in American literature.

152 pages   12 full color illustrations   clothbound, $9.95

Washington Irving's
Life of George Washington

with the original illustrations

Washington Irving's classic biography of George Washington, edited and abridged for the modern reader by Jess Stein, with 30 illustrations from steel engravings originally included in the separate volume, *Illustrations to Irving's Life of Washington*, published in New York in 1859.

An Introduction by Professor Richard B. Morris of Columbia University examines Washington Irving's warm, vivid portrait of his heroic namesake.

800 pages   30 illustrations   clothbound, $19.95

A Century of Commentary
on the Works of Washington Irving

edited by Andrew B. Myers

A collection of the most significant commentary on the life and works of America's first internationally successful author, Washington Irving.

Each of the forty-five selections, dating from 1860 to 1974, is introduced by noted Irving scholar Andrew B. Myers, who also provides a general introduction to the volume.

544 pages　　　　illus., chronology, index　　　　clothbound, $20.00

The Worlds of Washington Irving

edited by Andrew B. Myers

From a major exhibition of manuscripts, sketches, published works, and memorabilia of Washington Irving, presented at The New York Public Library.

More than 100 illustrations, selected and annotated by Andrew B. Myers, survey the varied worlds of Washington Irving: humorist, gentleman author, diplomat, country squire.

44 pages　　　　over 100 illus.　　　　cloth, $8.95　　　　paper, $5.50

Washington Irving: A Tribute

edited by Andrew B. Myers

Eight original essays by noted scholars on the life and works of Washington Irving.

86 pages   illus., bibliog.   hardcover, $3.95   paper, $2.95

The Knickerbocker Tradition:

Washington Irving's New York

edited by Andrew B. Myers

Six essays focusing on New York in Washington Irving's day examine political, social, and literary aspects of American culture.

160 pages   illus., bibliog., index   clothbound, $8.00

For further information, address the publisher:

Sleepy Hollow Restorations

150 White Plains Road
Tarrytown, New York   10591

[*Editor's Note:* In the nineteenth century, it was common practice for publishers to include in their books several pages listing other available publications. Sleepy Hollow Restorations has included such a list in this facsimile edition of *Bracebridge Hall* in keeping with the spirit of nineteenth century publishing traditions and to acquaint readers with other books which may be of interest.]

This facsimile edition of *Bracebridge Hall*, by Washington Irving, with illustrations by Randolph Caldecott, is based upon the First Edition originally printed by R. & R. Clark, Edinburgh, and published in late 1876 by Macmillan and Company of London.

The text and all of the one hundred eighteen illustrations originally executed by Randolph Caldecott and engraved by James D. Cooper, were reproduced with the greatest possible precision and printed by Aristographics, Inc., of New York City.

The binder's die, with which the cover of this facsimile edition was stamped, was carefully reproduced from a copy of the First Edition by Esquire Photo Engravers of New York City.

This facsimile edition was bound by The Haddon Craftsmen of Scranton, Pennsylvania.

The new Introduction by Andrew B. Myers to this facsimile edition was set in Linotype Old Style Number Seven, a type face specially selected to harmonize with the old style type employed for the First Edition.

Every effort has been made to reproduce the text, illustrations, and binding exactly as they appeared in the original.